CW01589995

Playing HOUSE

A SYDNEY SMOKE RUGBY NOVEL

Playing HOUSE

A SYDNEY SMOKE RUGBY NOVEL

AMY ANDREWS

Entangled Publishing, LLC
2614 South Timberline Road
Suite 105, PMB 159
Fort Collins, CO 80525
Visit our website at www.entangledpublishing.com.

Brazen is an imprint of Entangled Publishing, LLC. For more information on our titles, visit www.brazenbooks.com.

Edited by Liz Pelletier
Cover design by Fiona Jayde
Cover art from Wander Aguilar

Manufactured in the United States of America

First Edition February 2018

ENTANGLED
BRAZEN

For all the wallflowers.

Chapter One

Eleanor Davis had always felt like some kind of wildebeest in a family of gazelles, but tonight she was a wildebeest in a *herd* of the bastards. It was party time at the watering hole, and she was surrounded by gorgeous, preening animals.

Everyone sparkled and shone beneath the myriad fairy lights in the beer garden of one of Bungindally's oldest drinking establishments. Most of them had come to the outback town all the way from Sydney—twelve hundred kilometres east—for the annual city country rugby match, which had been played a few hours ago, and stayed on to celebrate her brother, Ryder's, engagement to Juliet.

But despite their city glamour, they seemed right at home in the middle of nowhere. Locals and sporting celebrities rubbed shoulders effortlessly, all laughing and indulging in animated conversations. They looked interesting and *interested* in each other, chatting away in their lively little groups as she watched from the sidelines next to a potted palm.

Part of Eleanor wanted to be amongst it all, but her heart

raced in a *bad* way at the thought. She was just too socially awkward, and frankly *boring*, to risk it.

She hadn't realised quite how boring until tonight.

A single, twenty-six-year-old woman still living with her parents on a cattle station in outer woop woop like some Jane Austen heroine. One who grew up with her head stuck in a book and preferred reading about nineteenth-century dating customs than swiping left. Who'd rather wear Victorian undergarments than red lacy thongs. Who spent her evenings moderating an online forum discussing bustles and corsets and etiquette in the court of Queen Victoria instead of hitting the local pub and talking to real people.

Yep. She was *that* boring. As compared to her sports star brother, who lived in Sydney and was leaving with his fiancée for Italy at the end of the footy season. Or her three gorgeous, social butterfly, *married* sisters.

Sadly, Eleanor's most intimate relationship was with her Elna. Unfortunately it was a sewing machine and *not* a Swiss vibrator, despite its multiple speeds and settings.

She'd been born in the wrong time—that was her problem. She was a nineteenth-century wallflower trapped in the age of Tinder.

No wonder she was still a virgin.

She was probably the oldest bloody virgin in Bungindally. Hell, probably the entire country. She was probably going to *die* the oldest virgin in Australia. Sigh.

Unless she settled. God knew the ratio of single men to women out here definitely ran in her favour. But she'd known all the eligible guys since childhood. Most of them were here tonight, and she called almost all of them her *mates*.

Her older sister, Lisa, teased Eleanor that she was waiting for Mr Darcy. To which she always replied, better Mr Darcy than Heathcliff. But was it so wrong to want to be swept off her feet by a tall, handsome stranger who'd romance her, *court* her, ask her father for her hand in marriage?

Eleanor glanced around again. Plenty of tall, handsome strangers around tonight, but none that seemed unattached *or* interested in a wallflower, for that matter.

She spied her brother, Ryder, standing with their parents and two of her three sisters. They were all remarkably alike—tall and fine boned. Even beneath Ryder's muscles there was a definite leanness to his skeletal makeup. Eleanor sighed, lamenting once again that she'd missed out on the Gallic genes and been burdened instead with the more robust traits from the Hungarian side of the family.

Eleanor's gaze fell on her future sister-in-law, who was standing with a small group of women she knew to be WAGS—wives and girlfriends—of the Sydney Smoke rugby players. More blessed creatures. So tall and thin and graceful.

One of them, Harper, was curvier but had the height to carry it off. Unlike herself, whose size twelve frame was completely disproportional. Wide hips, small waist, and boobs that, while on the big side, were not large enough to balance it all out. And, at five foot, she *definitely* lacked the height to carry any of it off.

Which was why she was wearing one of her own creations tonight. She'd made the bodice from a pattern based on a popular dress in London in the 1890s. It was low cut, made from a russet-coloured shot silk, the corset beneath emphasising her small waist while pushing up her cleavage.

The cap sleeves sat wide on her shoulders, clinging precariously to the notch of her collar bones. It was too sophisticated and classy for beer wench but walked that line with the expanse of décolletage on display.

She glanced down at her plumped-up cleavage. She *so* would have rocked the nineteenth century. If only she didn't like things such as personal hygiene and voting rights so damn much.

The rest of the dress was more modern, the skirt falling in a modest A-line to her knees—camouflaging her hips rather than emphasizing. She had contemplated going all the way and making the full outfit complete with bustle and floor-length skirt decorated with handmade satin roses and tiered frills, but people in town already thought she was kooky enough—no need to let the city folk in on it, too.

Not that Ryder or the rest of her family would have cared. They were well used to Eleanor and her fixation with everything nineteenth-century England. She could have worn a replica of Queen Victoria's wedding gown and none of them would have batted an eyelid, and she loved them for it.

They put up with her eccentricities because they were family and they were proud of how she'd turned her obsession into an online business. Making one-off, historically accurate gowns for people had started out as a hobby but had morphed into a profitable part-time job.

Unfortunately, not many people found it as endlessly fascinating as she did. In fact, most people's eyes tended to glaze over when she got started on her favourite topic.

Which was why she loved the online forum so much. People there understood her. They didn't find her boring or the subject dull. In fact, they could go back and forth about it on the screen all night. As long as the dodgy outback internet was playing nice.

But online people weren't real, as her middle sister, Jenny, kept telling her. They couldn't bow low over your hand, they couldn't ask you to dance the Cotillion, or hand you up into a carriage.

And they couldn't pop your cherry, either.

She had no idea why she was so damn fixated on her virginity tonight. Maybe it was the thick fugue of testosterone in the air.

Deep down she'd always considered her virginity—her *maidenhead*—a gift. Something to give to *the one*. Old-fashioned? Yes. But a steady diet of Georgette Heyer and Jane Austen had filled her head with romantic notions, and she'd been utterly swept away by the idea of *saving herself.*

She cringed at how unfeminist it was. But it wasn't like she thought *all* women should do the same. She couldn't care less how many men other women slept with, *she* wanted to wait. The problem was, there'd been no sign of *the one* in nearly a decade and her virginity was starting to feel more like a disease than a gift.

Technically, she doubted she actually still *was* a virgin. As far as presence of hymen went. She'd been riding horses since she was three, been using tampons since she was fifteen, and Carol, her third sister, had bought her a lipstick-sized vibrator for her eighteenth birthday which she'd run the batteries down on in a few days.

She was pretty sure that sucker had been worn away a long time ago.

But in all other ways, she was a virgin. With a capital *V.*

Fabulous. She was going to die a boring, spinster virgin. Probably at her sewing machine.

Peachy. *Just peachy.*

• • •

It'd been a long time since Bodie Webb—Spidey to his teammates—had fallen so completely and utterly in lust with a woman at first sight. And he met a *lot* of women. *Hot women* by anyone's standards. But being dumped by his long-term girlfriend over a year ago had left him cynical and jaded.

At the grand age of twenty-six.

The woman standing by herself near the far wall, trying to look invisible, had dragged him right out of his funk. Made him forget all about the slight groin strain he'd sustained during the game as well.

She was different. Not like the others. *Not like his ex.* She was hot all right but…softer, with hips and a waist Bodie could probably span with both his hands. And there was an air of uncertainty about her, like she'd rather be anywhere but here.

He, for one, was glad she wasn't.

And look at that, she didn't have a drink.

Bodie glanced around, trying to locate Ryder for an introduction because she sure as hell wasn't one of the Sydney entourage. But his best mate was laughing with his family and Bodie was more than capable of handling it himself.

He took a moment to straighten his tie before grabbing a glass of champagne and a schooner of beer off the tray of a passing waiter and heading in her direction. He didn't take his eyes off her as he made his way through the crowd, smiling politely as people greeted him but not stopping to chat. The closer he drew, the more he liked what he saw.

God, she was gorgeous. Soft and lush. And not just her boobs, although God almighty she had a cleavage he wanted to dive into. He'd been with busty women, but none of them had been soft and pillowy. They'd been high and firm, the sort that didn't move much of their own accord.

He'd bet his last cent he could bury his head in the cleavage he didn't seem to be able to take his eyes off and suffocate in all the plumpness. The same went for her mouth, all soft and full too. The closer he got, the more it seemed to scream *kiss me.*

He could get totally lost in that mouth.

It formed into a little *O* as he stepped out of the people milling in the middle of the beer garden and smiled at her. She'd obviously not been tracking his approach and her eyes, the colour of whiskey, widened in surprise. He swore he heard her quick intake of breath despite the loud murmur of conversation around them.

"Hi."

She blinked, clearly taken aback, sable lashes casting shadows on her cheekbones. A quick glance over her shoulder, as if to check it was her he was talking to, caused a funny little twist inside Bodie's chest.

What was wrong with the men around here?

Flyaway strands of her mahogany hair had escaped some kind of up-do to brush her practically bare shoulders, but he forced his gaze north because he didn't want to be some asshole who fixated on her chest. Her mouth was shiny with gloss the exact shade of her dress.

She didn't say anything, just continued to stare and seem as if she was trying to *become* the potted palm she'd taken a step toward.

He thrust the glass of fizzy liquid in her direction. "Champagne?"

He was usually smoother than this with women. But then, he hadn't ever really needed to do the talking. Women were good at that shit, plus he'd been in a committed relationship for a lot of years.

But damned if he didn't want to talk with this woman. This real woman. He hadn't realized until he'd seen her how many women he'd dated that had been all points and angles. Rail-like cheekbones, prominent ribs, coat hanger shoulders, stick-out hip bones, hard lacquered nails, bony spines.

All sharp angles, no curves. No softness.

She was regarding the glass of champagne like it might be laced with Rohypnol and him like he'd mistaken her for someone else. It was a refreshing change from women who eyed him hungrily like he was a hunk of meat. A life support system for a cock. A notch on a bedpost. Women who only wanted him for his rugby celebrity.

Or his trust fund.

He smiled again and waggled the champagne flute at her. "I could see you didn't have one, and being the only sober person at a party really sucks."

Bodie forced himself to keep his gaze trained on hers and not the ripe offering of her breasts being presented to his peripheral vision as if on a platter.

He *was not* some caveman who couldn't keep it in his pants.

She took the champagne, her fingernails—not short but not long, painted a soft pink—were pretty against the frosty glass. She opened her mouth to say something but stalled, instead raising the glass to her lips and gulping the champagne down in one hit.

Bodie smiled as she stared at the empty glass, obviously surprised at how quickly it had gone down. "Let me get you another."

"Oh no." She took a step closer and put her hand on his forearm.

For a brief moment, the aroma of orange blossoms enveloped him, then her hand slid from his as her cheeks went a very cute shade of pink. "I'll lose my inhibitions."

Bodie had always been with women who were bold and direct. Proudly *uninhibited*. Who knew shy and retiring was such a fucking turn on?

"In that case." He shot her a slow, easy smile, his gaze taking in her entire neckline before returning to her eyes. "I think we should *definitely* get you another."

A kind of strangled half breath escaped her lips, and he felt a similar hitch in his own breathing before his attention was snagged by a passing waiter. He swiped another champagne glass off the tray and passed it to her. "I'm Bodie. Bodie Webb. The guys call me Spidey."

• • •

Eleanor knew who he was. Her brother talked about Bodie a lot. They were practically best friends. It wasn't how she'd pictured him, though. Not that she'd really ever pictured anyone on her brother's team.

She was proud of Ryder and his stellar career, but, living all the way out here, she hadn't really followed it closely and frankly, rugby just wasn't her thing. She'd even taken a book to the game today.

Perhaps if she hadn't, she might have noticed Bodie sooner, even if the preppy guy in front of her didn't fit her preconceived ideas of a pro rugby player. Sure, he was tall, but then everyone seemed tall when you were five foot. And he was built. Eleanor could see the definition of his muscles beneath his snowy-white shirt and the fabric of his trousers.

But there was a clean cut appeal to him. Very white collar with his dirty blond hair trendily short at the back and sides, the longer bit on top artfully *jushed.* Not to mention his designer three-day growth manicured to within an inch of its dirty blond life.

He was more poster boy for Abercrombie and Fitch than the Sydney Smoke. Sure, the width of his shoulders told her he could play tough and dirty on the field, but give the man a pair of buckskin breeches and *hello, Mr Darcy.*

Was twenty-six too young to have a hot flush?

He was watching her, expectantly waiting for a reply, but Eleanor had completely forgotten what he'd said. Her body was in the middle of some kind of weird meltdown. Because a hot, tall, *sexy* rugby player was talking to her.

Flirting with her, if she wasn't very much mistaken.

She didn't know why he'd chosen her or why her heart was beating so rapidly or why her lungs felt like they weren't getting enough air. If this was the vapours, then it was no wonder smelling salts had been so damn vital in the nineteenth century.

Not that smelling salts would do much for the seditious whispers coming from her vagina.

Him. He's the one. Pick him!

God. Since when had her *vagina* started talking to her? Twenty-six years of silence and it chose tonight to go rogue? In front of this wickedly beautiful man?

What the hell was in that champagne?

"And you are?" he prompted.

There was a smile in his voice. Clearly, her inability to open her mouth and make words come out was amusing. She bet he had that affect on a lot of women. She took another sip of her champagne to find her voice.

And drown out the one between her legs still chanting *him, him, him.*

If she told him she was Nell, the name by which she was known, he'd probably know she was Ryder's sister. And then he might stop flirting with her. Hell, he might stop talking to her altogether what with all that bro code rubbish.

Unless she was some kind of bet.

Now *that* made sense. Why else would this outrageously sexy guy be flirting with her? Ryder had told her about Linc's bet over Em, so it sounded feasible. But surely Ryder wouldn't let the guys make a bet over his sister?

Unless he didn't know?

Whatever was going on here, bet or no bet, she wanted it to go on for longer. A twenty-six-year-old isolated-spinster-virgin had to take her opportunities where she got them.

She found her voice. "Eleanor."

It came out all breathy and ridiculous, but at least she'd managed to form a word. And it wasn't a lie, her name *was* Eleanor, even if no one ever called her by it. Ryder had called her Nell since she was born and it had stuck. Secretly, she'd always yearned to be called by her proper name—so much more regal than Nell—but siblings could be an uncooperative bunch.

"Eleanor." He rolled the name around his tongue. "It suits you."

He smiled at her and everything inside melted.

"I was named after my grandmother." And why on earth she'd told him that she had no idea.

He reached for her wrist lying limply by her side. "It's very nice to meet you, Eleanor."

He lifted her hand and bowed over it as he brought it to his lips and kissed her, his mouth warm and firm on her knuckles.

Oh. Dear. Lord.

Smelling salts! *Stat!* She really needed some smelling salts. She was swooning. Actually bloody *swooning.* A grown twenty-first century woman all weak-kneed while a wild party went on in her pants.

Him, him, him.

He straightened. Eyes the inky blue of twilight met hers. "How do you know Ryder?"

Eleanor froze, her brain scrambling for a response. No way was she telling him the truth. "Who doesn't know Ryder?"

Obfuscation was not a lie, she assured herself, as her vagina decided he was *definitely* the one and she should do something about it.

Her heart beat crazily at the thought of offering herself to Bodie. So what if he was Ryder's friend? It didn't need to be a big deal. There was a first time for everyone, right? And it wasn't like her father was going to insist on them getting married because Bodie had taken her *innocence.*

She couldn't believe she was even going there. But she was twenty-six. *It was time.*

Time for a good old-fashioned deflowering.

If he was willing, of course. But he *seemed* willing. He was flirting. *And* he was a man. A man who must surely have some serious game. All she needed to do was follow his lead. It would only take the once, after all. What was that term?

One and done.

She didn't even need an orgasm. Although she'd bet Bodie Webb gave *great* orgasms.

All she had to do was ask for it.

Right… Who was she kidding? As if she could just *ask*. She could barely have a conversation with the man. Plus virgins freaked guys out. She'd read that in a magazine at the local hairdresser.

The irony of that hadn't escaped her. *Not* being a virgin would have freaked guys out in the Victorian era.

Yep. She'd definitely been born in the wrong century.

"So you're local?"

Eleanor nodded, her face suddenly scarlet with the direction of her thoughts. She hated how easily she embarrassed in front of the opposite sex. She could castrate a paddock full of calves without a single blush, but talk to a man…

"Has anybody ever told you your eyes glow like a candle flame in whiskey? They're quite hypnotizing."

Eleanor almost sagged to the ground in relief at the lifeline he'd just offered her. Asking to be deflowered, *manoeuvring* a man to do so? She knew nothing. But she *did* know about hypnosis.

"Did you know that people in Victorian England were fascinated with hypnotists and all things occult?"

He gave a half chuckle and sipped his beer. "No, I did not." He leaned in a little closer. "Tell me more."

Growing in confidence, she did just that. "They'd go to these great halls to watch these shows where people would be hypnotized."

"With a pocket watch? You are in my power kind of thing?"

Eleanor's breath hitched at the thought of being in his power. "Something like that."

"You wouldn't need a watch to hypnotise me." His voice dropped an octave, and she found herself leaning in despite how much he flustered her. He lowered his mouth closer to her ear. "I'm already under your spell."

Part of Eleanor wanted to roll her eyes at what was a pretty cheesy pick up line. But she was under his spell, too.

"Would you like to…"

Throw me on your bed and deflower me?

Eleanor's pulse tripped at the daring it would take to come out and say *that*. Her hands trembled. Her breath stuck in her throat like gum. She *couldn't* say it.

But dear Lord he smelled *good*. Something sweet and subtle and clearly expensive.

Conscious of the nearby crowd, she screwed up her courage. "Go somewhere…quieter and I can…tell you more? I could tell you about a man called Fontaine who was famous for hypnotizing a lion at London Zoo."

His answering smile was wicked. "I thought you'd never ask."

Neither did she…

Chapter Two

Bodie couldn't believe his luck. He hadn't planned on getting laid tonight. The game they'd played had been brutal, and his groin still pulled occasionally. Plus, it was his best mate's night, and Bodie was on a break from all things female.

Unsurprisingly, sleeping with a bunch of women hadn't helped him get over his ex's betrayal a year ago.

But Eleanor's brand of shy eagerness had him totally hooked. She was like a breath of fresh air when he hadn't even realised he'd been deprived of oxygen.

He came from a family of sharks. Old money, private schools, overseas bank accounts. Generations of ruthless, sharp, mercenary businessmen. He'd been raised in a highly competitive environment, where the drive to win trumped everything else, and it had put him in good stead on the rugby field.

Anna, his ex, had come from that world, too, but it had still been a shock to realise their relationship had been just another business transaction.

The woman standing in front of him couldn't have been

any more different had he made her in a lab.

"Are you staying here?"

She nodded as if she didn't trust herself to speak. He held out his hand. "Shall we?"

She flushed as she glanced hastily around, obviously not keen to advertise their intentions. Bodie withdrew his hand and hoped like hell he hadn't blown it.

"How about I go up first, and you follow in about ten minutes?" she suggested.

Bodie wasn't used to being someone's dirty little secret—most women *bragged* over bagging a Sydney Smoke front rower. But she wasn't most women.

"It's a *very* small town," she murmured almost apologetically.

Bodie was an urban animal through and through, but he understood how easily reputations could be ruined, and she had to live here, not him. If she wanted it all secret squirrel, then he wasn't going to object.

Her secrecy was actually a plus. She was hardly likely to sell a story to some awful gossip rag if she didn't want to be seen leaving the party with him. "Whatever the lady wants."

He swore he heard a tiny little sigh deep in the back of her throat before she turned to leave. He smiled and shook his head. "What room number?"

She stopped, swung around, her cheeks almost scarlet now. "Twelve."

He nodded. "See you soon."

She started to turn away again but changed her mind and frowned at him instead. She chewed on her lip as if she was trying to decide something, and Bodie worried she was changing her mind.

"Maybe we should—" She glanced around, and Bodie could practically see the thoughts clashing around behind her expressive eyes. "Can we go to your room?"

He didn't give one fuck which room they used as long as he could sink into all that softness. Hell, even if she really *did* only want to talk about Victorian hypnotists, he'd be up for that, too.

Just being near this woman was a rush.

"Sure." He slipped his hand into his pocket and pulled out the old-fashioned key—no fancy swipe cards out past the black stump. "I'm in room eight."

She looked around again, her eyes darting here and there before quickly reaching for the key and hiding it with her palm.

"See you soon?"

The question and the uncertainty with which she'd delivered the question hit him square in the gut. He shot her his best *hell yes* smile. "I'll be there."

Wild horses couldn't keep him away.

• • •

Eleanor jumped at the knock. Her pulse spiked and the muscles of her neck contracted. Bodie had assured her he'd come, but here he was, on the other side of the door, and suddenly she was overwhelmed by the thought this was *really* happening.

It had been exactly three minutes since she'd let herself into his room. The entire trip upstairs, she'd been convinced she was going to run into somebody she knew and be delayed. A lot of locals had stayed in town for the night after the country/city match to celebrate their local boy's impending nuptials.

Which meant a lot of potential for gossip.

Thankfully, the staircase had been empty, as had the long corridor to the guest rooms. Now, all she had to do was go through with it. God…could she?

Yes. She could.

A second knock accelerated her pulse, and her gaze darted to the door a half-dozen steps away. She was going to have *sex.* Lose her virginity. Be *deflowered.*

She wished she'd had some more time to think about how it might go down, but all she'd had time for was snapping on the beside lamp, stripping off her clothes, and climbing into the white, hotel-supplied bathrobe she'd found hanging in the closet.

Just in case he thought she was *actually* here to talk about the occult practices of nineteenth century England.

Plus, the corset and bloomers she was wearing beneath her dress tended to slow down the disrobing process, and she didn't want that. It was hard to believe that a guy like Bodie was even *interested*, especially after prattling on about *hypnotising lions*, so she didn't want to make it any more difficult to do the deed.

A third knock. *Eep!* Was she actually doing this? A quiet, "Eleanor?" galvanized her out of her inertia.

Yes she was!

Without giving herself time to have a panic attack or chicken out, she practically tripped over her own toes getting to the door. She must have looked a flustered wreck as she yanked it open, her pulse in her neck pounding madly, but he didn't seem to notice as he pressed one big shoulder into the door frame and his gaze took a slow tour of her body.

It lingered where the gown crisscrossed the deep V of her cleavage before lifting to her face. "I wasn't sure you were going to open the door."

His voice tumbled over her smooth as water over river stones and *dear God*, the man smelled *good.* He towered over her as he lounged lazily in the doorframe. His gaze dropped to the rise of her breasts then back again. "I see you slipped into something more comfortable?"

Eleanor's cheeks heated, and her heart raced. Her instinct was to apologise for being so…forward. But damn it, she hadn't come here to play Scrabble or admire the recent refurbishment to the accommodations. This was operation *losing it.*

She drew in a shaky breath. "Yes."

He smiled. "May I come in?

Eleanor's knees wobbled at the request. This was *his* room, and she was clearly naked beneath the gown, but the fact that he was asking her permission to enter hit her in all her nineteenth-century feels.

Bodie may have been an elite rugby player, but the man had *manners.* And manners made Eleanor swoon like crazy.

If he wasn't careful, she'd fall in love with him.

She grabbed him by the tie and yanked him inside.

He didn't need any more encouragement, and Eleanor vaguely heard the door clicking shut as the hardness of his body smooshed up against the softness of hers. She pushed up on her tippy toes, seeking his mouth, and he met her halfway.

She moaned at the first touch of his lips, uncaring how much of a rookie she sounded. She was electrified by the feel of him and intoxicated by his taste and smell. His whiskers prickled and teased and she moaned again, her hands grabbing hold of his biceps as the earth tilted on its axis.

"Christ." He pulled away, his chest heaving as he stared down at her, his inky gaze satisfyingly bewildered. "You taste so good. I want to *feast* on you all night."

Eleanor barely had time to register the feral lust turning his looks from preppy to predatory before his mouth was back on hers, hot and hard. He hauled her up his body, his hands gripping the backs of her thighs, lifting her feet off the ground, urging her legs apart.

Her gown gaped below the tie as her ankles locked tight around his waist, and Eleanor clung to him, oblivious of all else *but* him. Sucking in his taste and his scent, the rough chug of his breath and the deep rumble of his groan. Nothing mattered but the sweet plunder of his mouth, the heat of his belly pressed into the soft flesh of her inner thighs and the hardness of muscles beneath his skin.

She didn't register him moving, his long sure strides efficiently eating up the distance between the door and the bed without tripping or missing a step despite having a fully grown woman wrapped around him. She didn't even register falling or the soft embrace of the mattress as they landed. Or the fact her ankles stayed locked tight.

She *did* register the delicious weight of his body, the way his hips settled into the cradle of hers and the steel of his erection at the bare juncture of her thighs.

Oh yeah baby. Her vagina was all over that.

He broke off the kiss, and Eleanor mewed a protest, reaching for him again, sliding her hands behind his neck, trying to tug him down. He resisted with a smile, his hand going to the tie at her waist as he rolled his torso to the side a little.

His gaze locked with hers. "I need to look at you."

Eleanor's pulse tapped madly as he tugged it, swallowing to wet her parched throat. This was it. A man was going to see her naked. She'd always thought she'd be shy or embarrassed in this moment, but the desire in his gaze, the huskiness in his voice, held her in his thrall.

He *wanted* to see her. And she wanted him to see.

"The second I saw you across the room, I wanted to get you naked." Eleanor's belly tightened. "I wanted to peel you out of that dress and sink my face into your gorgeous, soft tits."

Her nipples hardened at his guttural use of language.

"So soft," he whispered.

As a C cup, she knew she wasn't small-breasted, but she'd

always wished for perkier. Less…jiggly. Although Bodie, apparently, didn't agree.

He pushed the edges of the gown apart and looked his fill. Cool air was a delicious torture against the puckered tips of her nipples. The expression of raw desire on his face tightened things much *lower* and a warm ooze slicked her inner thighs.

His gaze returned to her face. "You're beautiful."

His low husky whisper, full of reverence, almost made her cry. No man had ever told her she was beautiful.

Or looked at her like she was.

True, she'd never been naked in front of one, either, but her heart swelled the same way it did at the end of a really good romance novel.

It was probably just the grateful-to-be-losing-it-virgin thing transferring some kind of significance to his words because he was the first. But she couldn't have scripted her first time better.

And they hadn't even got to *penetration*.

His hand slid from her waist to cup first one breast then the other, his stare seemingly transfixed as his fingers trailed slowly over all their contours. Her skin goosed beneath his touch and a strangled moan escaped as he teased the tight achy points of her nipples.

Her hips circled involuntarily, bumping against the thickness of his erection, rubbing against it, trying to ease the throb intensifying between her legs. She might never have done this before, but her body knew what it wanted and how to get it.

She needed him inside her. *Now.*

"Bodie…" She circled again. "Please."

He shot her a lazy smile. "What's your rush?"

The clench of his jaw and the unevenness of his breath gave him away, though. He was obviously as affected as her but seemed determined to keep teasing rather than getting down to business.

And she really, *real*ly needed him to get down to business. They could *play* later.

"Bodie. I need..." She didn't know how to come out and tell him what she needed. Getting to this stage had been ballsy enough.

He lowered his mouth to hers, almost touching but not quite. "I know what you need." His mouth was a gossamer brush on hers as he spoke, his warm breath flowing over her lips.

Then he dipped his head and sucked a nipple deep into the back of his throat. Eleanor gasped at the sudden move, crying out as his tongue joined in the action and the suction got harder, walking the line between pleasure and pain.

The sensation slugged her right between her legs. Right where it was already impossibly sensitive, where she was strung so tight that each flick of his hard tongue was like a direct jolt to her clitoris.

Christ. She did *not* need that.

If she orgasmed *now* how would that look? Nothing screamed virgin like a stealth climax before the main event. He might start to wonder about her level of experience. He might even guess this was her first time. And what if he freaked out? What if he didn't want to take it all the way?

"*Bodie*."

If it sounded like she was begging, she didn't care. She couldn't take the sensation anymore. It sizzled like static in every cell, stimulating her beyond all control. Her pulse was racing, her throat was so parched it rasped like two pieces of sandpaper rubbing together.

She grabbed his head and pulled his mouth off her, a wet elongated nipple slipping from his lips. "Later."

She reached for his tie and had it off in seconds. Her

fingers landed on his buttons, fumbling with them uselessly until a crazed brain cell—or maybe it was her damn talking vagina—urged her to pull the shirt apart with her bare hands.

Which was exactly what she did.

Buttons pinged against the headboard and she stilled momentarily, shocked at her audacity. “Sorry.”

He laughed. “It’s okay, I have another one.”

Relief flowed through her system and her shock was quickly forgotten as his chest filled her vision. And dear *God*, what a chest. Broad and smooth. Warm and golden. Defined pecs, brown nipples, flat abs. An *eight pack*, to be precise. She counted to be sure. And no hair except a narrow trail leading from his belly button.

Bodie Webb didn’t need a pocket watch. Not when he could just whip his shirt off and hypnotise every woman in a city block into clucking like a chicken or whatever the hell else he wanted.

She lifted her head and planted tiny kisses from the flat of a nipple all the way to his neck. “Your chest should be bronzed and mounted,” she said against the pulse in his throat.

“Ditto.” He chuckled but there was a rough quality to it as her mouth closed over the thick beat and she sucked.

Desperate for more, Eleanor’s hands delved between their bodies, finding his fly, dealing with his belt buckle and the button, grasping for the zip all while the rough pant of his breathing filled her head.

Her fingers brushed his erection. He groaned but she didn’t linger, just ripped the zip down. She was on fire, eager to get her hands on it in the flesh. Eager to feel it inside her.

With the zip undone, she pulled at his trousers, frantic to get them off. But her fingers were all trembly and useless, and she whimpered in frustration.

He chuckled into her neck, his breath warm. “Slow

down."

She ignored him, managing through sheer frustrated-virgin will to coordinate her fingers, finally easing his trousers off his hips, shoving her hands into his underwear at the back and peeling both his trousers and his briefs down together before doing the same at the front, his hot, hard erection finally in her grasp.

His quick, harsh intake of breath and his long slow, "*Fuuuuuuck*," on exhalation was gratifying on levels Eleanor never even knew existed.

He was big and thick and it was tempting to palm him, to take the time to explore every inch of his velvety hardness, but she was too close to her goal to get sidetracked. She could only think of one thing as she rotated her hips again, positioning him in the general vicinity of where she wanted him, where she was hot and wet and needy.

Where it ached and begged and bitched for possession.

She let go of his girth, grabbed his hips, shut her eyes tight and whispered, "Now," as her pulse hit about two hundred beats per minute and she lectured herself to *relax*.

The rest was up to him.

He huffed another laugh into her neck. "Patience." She opened her eyes as he eased up a little, supporting himself on forearms flattened either side of her head. "We've got all night and I want to explore *all* your body first. Maybe even—" He smiled in a very sexy, self-deprecating way. "Take *all* my clothes off?"

Eleanor didn't give a fig about his state of dress. She didn't care that his pants were only half down or his buttonless shirt was still on his back or his shoes and socks were still firmly on his feet. She had all the equipment that mattered at her fingertips.

"Bodie…*please*." She licked her lips and his eyes widened and she lifted her head off the bed and kissed him long and deep and as dirty as someone who'd only ever kissed three guys knew how.

He was panting hard when she pulled away. So was she.

"It's been a…while for me." A *loooong* while. Twenty-six years, to be exact.

She hoped like hell she wasn't about to be struck down for not being entirely truthful. Not before it was over, anyway.

"And all I need right now is to feel you—"

She reached between them again and wrapped a hand around his steely girth. He groaned and shut his eyes momentarily. Eleanor bit back a whimper at the thought of it pumping in and out.

"Inside me."

He swooped down and kissed her long and deep and as dirty as a man who'd probably kissed more women than they both had fingers and toes for.

So dirty.

He pressed his forehead to hers when he was done, his uneven breath mixing with hers. "Okay then." He flexed his hips, sliding his erection through the slick folds of her sex. "But only because I want to be inside you so fucking bad."

Eleanor almost sobbed in relief as she quickly, *greedily* palmed his exposed ass with one hand and angled him towards her core, notching him against her, pressing into him urgently.

"Wait, wait." His biceps trembled and he sucked in a breath as if he was fighting to maintain control. "Condom."

It came out on some kind of tortured grunt but *Jesus…* condoms, *of course*, what was she thinking?

But she needn't have worried. He was reaching behind him, groping for his trousers and what she presumed was his wallet. Yes, his wallet appeared suddenly and from out of it he pulled a square foil packet. He grinned and said, "Boy Scout," before ripping it with his teeth and, with a startling economy of movement, rolled it on without breaking eye contact once.

"Now..." He grinned again. "Where was I?" One flex of his hips brought the thickness of his head right to her centre.

Eleanor's breath caught at the blunt pressure, her pulse skyrocketing. "Right there." She slid her arms around his neck, the frantic thrum of her heartbeat growing louder in hers as he lowered his body on top of hers.

"Yes," he muttered, his breathing unsteady, "right there."

Chapter Three

Eleanor gasped at the thick intrusion as he groaned and said, "*God yes, there,*" and thrust halfway in.

It wasn't painful, she was so wet his erection had glided in easily. But it was full—*really* full. She felt impossibly stretched. In a *good* way.

If this was possession, she was already a fan.

"You okay?"

Okay? She couldn't have been any more okay if she'd been in the middle of a nineteenth-century orgy.

"Yes…please." She fought to steady her breathing as she slid her hands to his upper arms. "Don't stop."

His biceps flexed beneath her fingers, and he slid all the way home on a groan that rumbled right down to her toes and back up again. Eleanor eeked out a breath, her body absorbing the shock of being filled so completely, stretched to her limits.

She'd done it. She was no longer a virgin.

She'd been deflowered.

And bloody hell…it had been worth the wait. Not only

had she lost it to a man who had kissed her hand, called her a lady, and acted like a perfect gentleman, but he was hotter than a calendar full of naked French rugby dudes.

His biceps flexed again and she squeezed her thighs tight around his hips and ass to keep him still. "Wait, wait," she whispered.

Bodie let out a half laugh, half strangled groan. "Now she wants to go slow."

Eleanor chuffed out a laugh, too, sliding her hands under his shirt to his back, anchoring them against his shoulder blades. "Just hold there for a moment." She needed to catch her breath for a second, to adjust. "I want to feel you."

And she wanted to remember it forever. The way Bodie felt inside her those seconds after taking her virginity. He didn't seem to mind, kissing her eyes and her neck and her ears and her cheeks with such sweetness and gentleness she almost wanted to cry.

He kissed her mouth then, long and slow and deep, and she got lost in it, consumed by the glide and play of it. She didn't know when he started moving, only that she slowly became aware of the rock of his hips, the shift of ass beneath her calves, the steady flare of friction in the muscles that cradled him deep inside her.

A moan spilled from her lips, a groan spilled from his.

"Jesus." His mouth broke away and he was panting as he pressed his forehead against hers. "You're so fucking tight."

It probably wasn't right how much his language turned her on. But *Lordy,* it turned her on. She wasn't a prude about swear words. She'd grown up around a bunch of rough and tumble jackaroos whose cursing was as inventive as it was frequent. She'd just preferred the art of subtle insult perfected in historical times to more coarse expressions.

Which only proved that, despite years of having her head buried in books, she knew zip about language.

Damned if she didn't want to tell him she mightn't feel so tight if he wasn't so *fucking* big. But she'd pushed enough boundaries tonight. Plus she wasn't sure if she could even form a coherent sentence at the moment.

He was withdrawing almost completely now and plunging back in again, and she was so full and tight and achy she wasn't sure how much longer she could take it.

It was too, *too* much.

She moaned and shook her head from side to side, agitated by the intensity, overwhelmed by the building pressure, her pulse hammering through her head. She was on the edge of something big, something hovering just out of reach, retreating a little with every withdrawal, inching closer with every thrust.

She could hear the frustrated mewling animal noises in her throat and then his mouth was pressed to her ear, and he was whispering, "I know, baby, I know," as his hand reached between their bodies and his fingers found her clitoris and stroked hard and sure.

It was exactly what she needed. The sudden stimulus was like a pin to a balloon, popping all the pressure in one almighty rush.

She cried out, gasping for air, her short, neat nails raking hard down his back as she trembled beneath him, freefalling through a rainbow of pleasure, colours washing over her in waves, flaring bright and tangible, stroking like velvet over her body before rippling away to be taken by another, more intense than the last.

"Jesus, *yes*." Bodie groaned in her ear as he pounded into her, his shoulders hunching into the action, tossing her higher and higher into the rainbow with every thrust, ripping a long continuous moan from her mouth. "Christ…" His buttocks clenched tight beneath her calves, the muscles in his back and biceps trembling. "I'm coming."

The announcement was torn from his throat as was his shout of release, splintering over her into a thousand shards of pleasure, prolonging her orgasm. The quiver of his muscles and his ragged pants were like a chant in her ear as he drove them both to their completion before finally collapsing on top of her.

Bodie's breath rushed noisily in and out right near her ear. "Fuck. Me."

Eleanor laughed huskily as she struggled for her own breath under the weight of a six-foot rugby forward. She doubted Jane Austen could have put it better. It had been fast and furious, more grunt than finesse, but she was no longer virgin territory.

And what a way to raise a flag!

Was sex *always* like that? Something *more* than physical? She'd expected it to be a bump and grind. A meeting of bits. A genital party. She hadn't been prepared for a total body experience. To feel it in her heart, her mind, her soul.

Eleanor stifled a gasp as he eased off her, sliding from her body. She felt surprisingly bereft at his departure, despite it being easier to breathe. But then he settled on his back beside her, his fingers twining with hers, and her heart did a funny little giddy up.

"I hope our neighbours aren't in because I reckon we've got about five minutes before the cops kick the door down to check you haven't been murdered."

Eleanor laughed at the absurdity. So did he. She rolled her head to the side and inspected his profile, admiring the hard blade of his jaw and the sharp line delineating his three day growth from the hollow beneath his cheekbone. "Sorry. I was kinda loud, wasn't I?"

He rolled his head to the side, too. Her heart did another little giddy up as their gazes met. Her cheeks heated, suddenly shy despite what they'd just done. "Don't be sorry. Nothing like a bit of vocal appreciation to make a man feel like king of the world. Besides…" A slow smile spread over his features. A smile that stroked right between her legs. "I wasn't exactly mute."

That was very true. His loss of control had been extremely gratifying.

He raised his head off the bed, looking down at clothes that looked like they'd been through a cyclone. "Don't go anywhere. I'll be right back." He kissed her quick and hard. "We're not done here."

Muscles that had clamped tight around Bodie as he'd thrust inside her tightened again at his sexy pronouncement. The glimpse of his ass before he yanked his trousers up didn't help.

Prior to having her world rocked, Eleanor would have been more than happy to gather her clothes and leave after the deed had been accomplished. *One and done.* But she really wanted to do *that* again.

It'd been far too good *not* to repeat.

She did get up, however, and pull back the bedclothes. An unfamiliar ache down low reminded her she'd used some new muscles tonight, and she smiled to herself in secret delight as she shrugged out of the fluffy gown and crawled between the bed sheets.

Nervous suddenly at his return, she wasn't sure how she should present herself. How should she lie? On her back? On her side with her hair down and her lips all pouty?

Sheets on or off?

The wedge of light spilling from the bathroom flicked out and Eleanor quickly lay back, pulling the sheets to her shoulders. Her pulse leaped as Bodie appeared, gloriously, completely, unashamedly naked.

He clearly hadn't had any issues deciding on presentation.

She tracked his progress as he crossed to the bed. Her

stupid cheeks heated again as she tried desperately to be cool and not ogle the man like a sex-starved nymphomaniac but *good Lord*, he was magnificent, how could she not?

His bronzed skin, his well-defined quads, the *eight* perfect pillows of his abs, his long easy stride. And his…member.

That was the word that sprung to mind, the terminology she was used to from many, many historical romance novels. But the piece of anatomy in question, still impressively thick despite its flaccid state, was far too conceited for such a genteel euphemism. And penis was too anatomical.

Her brain tripped over other words. Manhood. Phallus? Prick? Dick? *Cock.* Yes, cock was the word for it, sitting there all proud and pleased with itself. *As it bloody should be.*

Not that she'd probably ever mutter the word out loud.

She blushed some more as he pulled the sheets back and slid in beside her. "Good." He smiled at her as he shuffled close, her abdominals jumping as his hand glided onto her belly beneath the sheets. "You didn't run away."

Of course not. *Did she look like she'd taken leave of her senses?* "How could I when there's so much more knowledge to impart about Victorian hypnotists?"

He chuckled, and she almost sighed in relief. She probably should have said something like *would you try and catch me.* But she'd never really learned the art of flirting, so she was going to have to fall back on her comfort zone—flippancy.

He settled on his side against her, trapping her arm between them, his leg warm along the length of her thigh, his foot brushing against hers. His *cock* was pressed into her hip precariously close to her hand, and she curled her fingers into her palm to stop herself from groping him.

He bent his arm up and supported his head with his hand as he gazed down at her. "That was…" He smiled again and shook his head. He seemed to be as lost for words as she was and Eleanor's heart squeezed as he dropped a kiss on her shoulder.

"Yeah." Her gaze met his. "It was."

The hand that had been sitting on her belly slid north until it was free of the sheets, his fingers brushing up her neck to toy with her mouth, tracing her bottom lip. "You have a sexy mouth."

"So do you." He had an uptilt to his lips as if he was ready to laugh at a moment's notice.

Or kiss someone breathless.

His fingers trailed south again, down her neck, onto her chest, slowly revealing more and more of it as he drew lazy circles, his gaze following the progress. Her breath hitched and her nipples grew into hard little pebbles as the sheet inched slowly down, revealing the swells of her breasts.

He lifted his gaze and smiled at her, an index finger stopping at the dip of her cleavage. "I love this V here." He traced his finger up the swell of one breast, then the other, before hooking a finger into the sheet and tugging.

Bodie's breath hissed out appreciatively as the cool air hit her exposed nipples. It took all Eleanor's willpower not to grab the sheet and cover herself. Having him look at her in the throes of passion was one thing, having him stare at her in the aftermath seemed a little more clinical.

Even if he did look like he wanted to lick beer off them.

His hand moulded first one, then the other, with the concentration of a sculptor moulding clay. He glanced at Eleanor. "I don't understand why you don't just lay in bed all day playing with these babies."

It was said rather reverently but the visual was funny as hell and she laughed. "I can just imagine telling the jackaroos to go on ahead and muster without me because I wanted some quality time with my boobs."

"Trust me, they'd understand." He returned his attention to the caress of his hand. "I could look at these all night."

He dipped his head, running his tongue from one nipple all the way across to the other.

Eleanor moaned. It rose in her throat, full and needy, pushing against her vocal chords and slipping straight out. She couldn't have stopped it any more than the sudden rush of slickness coating her inner thighs.

Her hand fell to the crown of his head, tunnelling into the longer hair on top, holding him there as he lingered over each nipple. Abruptly, he pulled away, his gaze, satisfyingly unfocused, locked with hers.

"Are you hungry?"

Eleanor's head was spinning from the sexual storm he'd created, and he wanted to talk food? How could he think about food? *Now?* "Ummm… No."

"I'm *starving*," he said, his hand absently stroking a fully aroused nipple.

"Right…well." She shook her head to clear the sexual fog. "I think they do some basic room service." Although she'd have to leave right now because she knew everyone who worked at the hotel.

Or there was the mini bar. Would expensive chocolate bars and little bottles of alcohol suffice?

He grinned at her apparent confusion. "I didn't mean for food."

And he tugged the sheets all the way down, sliding his body over the top of hers, kissing the midpoint between her breasts before heading south, his hot tongue leading the way. It was hard to gather her thoughts as his head slowly disappeared.

To her belly button. And further still…

It was then she realized his intended target. "No." Her heart rate spiked, her hands flew into action, inserting themselves between his face and her pelvis, crossing them over to form a barrier.

He glanced up, a smile playing on his mouth as he rested his chin on the back of her upper hand, his fingers digging lightly into the flesh of her hips. He cocked an eyebrow. “You don’t like?”

Eleanor would love to have an opinion to express, but given she’d never had a guy go *down there*, she was a novice. She’d heard a whole lot of sisterly girl talk about it and consumed enough media to be intrigued. The material she’d read on pornography in the nineteenth century and the photographs she’d stumbled across when researching lingerie of the era had left her positively agog.

But she wasn’t exactly well…*groomed*. She’d never really seen the point. Who was there to care out here? The cattle didn’t care whether she had a Brazilian or not. And she didn’t think in an area where males significantly outnumbered females that the men in these parts would be terribly picky.

But she’d read enough gossip magazines to know that city women took care of that shit.

“It’s not exactly…” Dear Lord, she did not want to be having this conversation. His warm breath flowed over her hands and whispered against her belly. “*Vagazzled* down there, if you know what I mean. I wasn’t expecting…”

Crazy hot rugby sex.

Hell, if she’d known what the gods-of-good-long-suffering-virgins had in mind for her tonight, she’d have buffed her muff until it shone.

“You,” she ended lamely.

He laughed. “Vagazzled?”

Eleanor blushed. That was the word all the *in* people were using, wasn’t it? She’d read it in a magazine somewhere. The familiar frustration at being out of step with her contemporaries stirred all her nerd girl insecurities.

“You can laugh.” She huffed out a breath. “But I’d bet my last cent the type of women you usually—” God…she couldn't even say it.

"Go down on?"

Eleanor didn't bother to confirm or deny, she just ploughed on, wanting the embarrassment to end. "Are all waxed and...bejewelled."

"Vagazzled *and* bejewelled." Laughter shone in his eyes.

God, where was a decent-sized hole to fall into when you needed it?

"Au naturel might have been all right in the eighteen hundreds, but not today. And I hate to break this to you, but I can't exactly walk into the one and only beauty therapist here in town, who, by the way, *knows my mother and plays the piano at church every Sunday*, and ask for my pubic hair to be fashioned into a landing strip. Monica is sixty-three, it would probably give her a heart attack. She thinks a bikini wax is a mortal sin."

He didn't bother holding his laughter back anymore, belly laughing with gusto. His warm breath caressed her stomach, goose bumps breaking across her flesh in its wake.

"I'm sorry." He half choked, trying to rein in his laughter. "I'm picturing how Monica might take it if a dude walked in and asked for some manscaping?"

Eleanor snort laughed. "I'm pretty sure there'd be some holy water involved."

They laughed together this time but, when it settled, they were still back at square one, her hands still crossed in front of herself. He nuzzled the back of her hand for a moment before his gaze wandered up her body and settled on her face. His fingers crept from her hips to her wrists, attempting to gently prise them apart.

Eleanor locked them tight.

"Open Sesame." The low authoritative streak to his voice and the steady, determined glint in his eyes breathed life into the pulse beating between her legs. "I promise you won't regret it."

Eleanor swallowed. She didn't doubt it for a minute. "Maybe I should just go and have a quick shower?"

She'd showered just prior to the party but she had experienced a mind blowing orgasm since then. Things were not only a little overgrown but a little…*slippery*, too. *She* could smell the aroma of their sex clinging to her skin and the musk of her arousal floating on the air.

Surely he'd appreciate it a little less *perfumed* down there?

"Fuck no." His instant gravelly denial was sexy as hell. "I'm already salivating for you."

To prove his point he pushed his nose at her closed fingers and inhaled deeply before raising his head again and looking at her with a steady, steely determination. "And if you think I'm letting you up from this bed, then you're crazy."

He tugged her hands again, and again she resisted. A small knowing little smile—sexy as hell—heated things up behind her belly button and between her thighs. "There are two things I do really well, Eleanor. One is tackle, the second is giving head. Trust me, you don't want to be on the receiving end of the first but you *do* want to be on the receiving end of the second."

It was breathtakingly conceited, but damn if it didn't turn her thighs to jelly and melt her resistance like a blowtorch to an ice cube. Hell yes she wanted the second.

Her breath hitched as he tugged again and this time she let her hands fall away. That small smile broadened as the barriers to his further sexual exploration disappeared. "Good choice." He held her eyes for a beat longer before dropping his gaze.

Eleanor's heart pounded as he stared at her, his gaze fixed so intensely she wanted to squirm. "Now that's what I'm talking about," he half whispered, half muttered, his low breath caressing the flesh of her inner thighs. He shifted down some more to get a closer look, his shoulders easing between her legs, parting them wider.

"So pretty."

Her cheeks heated as he continued to look his fill and when she couldn't stand it a second longer, she reached over and flicked out the light. His warm chuckle vibrated against her slick folds, and she shivered.

"I don't need the light, honey, I can make you come like this blindfolded with both hands tied behind my back."

Eleanor had *no* doubt. Just as she had no doubt that she'd orgasm in about ten seconds flat. But she'd come a long way tonight and was so far out of her comfort zone she might as well be on another planet. Bodie doing *this* to her as well seemed downright greedy and thoroughly, wickedly debauched.

It seemed like it should be done in a very dark room.

Eleanor was so tense, waiting for his mouth, her muscles were at screaming point. The warm flow of his breath stirred her flesh, and she bit back a whimper as she ground her pelvis into the bed instead of his face.

He made a noise that was half groan, half growl. "Jesus, you smell intoxicating."

The taut string of Eleanor's anticipation snapped. She wasn't a woman who was pushy in bed. Clearly—she'd been a virgin until half an hour ago! And being introverted meant she didn't usually push for what she wanted. But if he didn't stick his tongue where he'd been boasting he was going to stick it very soon, she was going to spontaneously combust.

Her heart hammered as she dared to push. "Why are you still talking?"

She registered his low laugh for two seconds before he buried his face between her legs and her pulse shot into the stratosphere.

"*Bodie!*" His name was torn from her throat as his tongue immediately found its mark, pressing hard and relentless over the screamingly sensitive bundle of nerves.

This was no gentle exploration, no slow tease, no lazy build. This was quick and hard and fast. This was about the destination, *not* the journey, and Eleanor sunk her nails into the balls of his shoulders and hung on for dear life.

She panted and moaned, writhing against his face, his hands two hot brands holding her hips in place. Every time she jerked in his hold, he held tighter, pressing his tongue harder until the first ripple of pleasure hit the back of her thighs in very short order.

"Oh…God…*Bodie*."

He didn't reply, groan in encouragement, or lift his head. He just doubled down, sucking the taut bead beneath his tongue into his mouth. Eleanor cried out as the hard edge of his teeth proved just the right stimulus to trip her into the fullness of her climax.

Pulse hammering through her skull, she sunk her nails into his shoulders, gasping as the hot wave of pleasure flushed between her legs before rolling through her pelvis and buttocks and belly. It exploded like fireworks and sizzled like lightning through her system. Popping and fizzing, leaving her spineless, leaving her breathless, leaving her dazzled.

Leaving her spent.

Leaving her wondering how in the hell she was going to live without having Bodie and his magic tongue on tap.

Chapter Four

Bodie woke the next morning with a smile on his face and a dick hard enough to smash diamonds. Unfortunately, he was also alone. The thought Eleanor might just be in the bathroom was comforting until he rolled to his side and felt how cool the sheets beside him were.

Nothing but the lingering trace of orange blossom.

Well *shit*...that wasn't how he'd planned on waking this morning. He'd wanted to feel her soft, warm body draped against his. He'd wanted to touch and stroke her in the morning light filtering in around the edges of the heavy hotel curtain. He wanted to bury himself inside her one last time, then figure out how soon she could get to Sydney and see him so they could do it all over again.

He laughed out loud. It was absurd to be feeling so damn...*giddy* about a woman after such short acquaintance, but Eleanor had made a lasting impression—and he wasn't just talking about the nagging pull in his groin or the nail marks on his back and shoulders.

Although a woman who came loud enough to shatter the

windows in the room did tend to swell a man's head.

Both of them.

It was her softness and her lack of…guile that drew him. Her genuine surprise at his interest and her nervous prattle about Victorian hypnotists made him smile even now. It had been a long time since he'd been with *anyone* who didn't want *something* from him. Who didn't even seem to know who he was.

And that could be seriously addictive.

Bodie rolled on his back with a sigh, ignoring the persistent erection demanding to be serviced. How it was so damn perky this morning after last night's smorgasbord, he had no idea.

He smiled to himself as he thought about laughing and talking with her into the night, the darkness and post-coital euphoria encouraging her to relax and open up. She told him about her lifelong obsession with everything Victorian, her collection of books on the monarch and the era as well as her collection of historical romance novels. And all about *Queen Victoria's Closet*, her online vintage dressmaking business.

He'd talked about rugby. A much easier subject than anything more personal, although rugby *was* pretty damn personal. She seemed conversant enough in it to make conversation, but she didn't ask him about his stats or his pay cheques or his endorsements.

Which was a breath of fresh air.

Instead, she asked him what else he would have done had he not played footy for a living, and if he was ever scared on the field, and how often his body hurt. Hell, not even his *mother* had asked him if his body hurt.

A *real* breath of fresh air.

And to have a conversation with a woman where his net worth and his rich-ass family weren't mentioned was so damn good he'd kissed her for it at one stage and then they hadn't spoken for quite some time.

In fact, they'd had sex two more times, because keeping his hands off her had proved to be impossible and she'd been so damn eager.

Bodie rolled out of bed and headed for the bathroom, wondering about tracking her down. He made a mental note to ask Ryder about her. If she was local, too, and lived out his way then Ryder must know her.

He stood at the vanity and inspected himself in the mirror, his gaze drawn to the livid scratch marks on his left shoulder. He twisted around to view his back, noting the double set of scratches, one on either side of his rib cage. They'd all scabbed and the skin around the edges had pulled taut.

Man. She'd really dug in there. Like his groin strain, he'd barely felt them at the time, but they were tender this morning.

His stomach growled and he headed out to the main room to dress.

Maybe Eleanor was downstairs eating. You never knew your luck in a small town, right?

He saw the note as soon as he neared the bedside table, and his heart skipped a beat as he grabbed the paper and sunk onto the mattress. It was written in a beautiful, feminine flowing script that could almost be calligraphy, and it made him happy just looking at it.

Nothing bad could be delivered in such a pretty hand, surely?

Bodie,

Thank you so much for last night. I had an incredible time. You are an amazingly generous lover and I will never forget the hours I spent in your arms.

I only ask that you don't tell anyone what happened between us. I know guys like to brag, but I feel that my brother, in particular, may not be so keen on a blow by blow.

Goodbye and thank you. I will always remember the day the city came to the country.

Eleanor (Nell) Davis

Bodie blinked. Apparently, pretty writing *could* pack a real punch. Like a sledgehammer to the gut.

Holy. Fuck.

Eleanor was *Nell?* Nell Davis. *Ryder's sister, Nell.*

He'd slept with his best friend's sister?

Jesus. He was going to hell. *Best-friend's-sister-fucking hell.* He'd broken the code. Unwritten. Unspoken. But very fucking ingrained. You didn't bone a teammate's ex. Or his mother.

Or his *sister.*

Pretty simple rules, really. And no real hardship. There were plenty of women out there more than willing to be with a rugby superstar. Steering clear of a few was no problem. And yet, somehow, Bodie had managed to screw it up.

Jesus.

Disbelief was starting to morph into irritation as unease pitched through his stomach. Why the fuck hadn't she told him who she was? The warm buzz that had flowed through his veins since he'd woken evaporated. Every thought and feeling he'd had about Eleanor melted away. *She'd* known who he was all along.

Had she been playing him?

She *had* to know what this would do to his and Ryder's friendship if it was to come out. What that kind of disruption could do to the team dynamic. Had she put on some clueless female act so she could sink her hooks into him? Was he some kind of ticket to the city for her?

He hadn't got that vibe, but…

Another thought, born from the gnawing worry that had been there since Anna had left, struck. Did she know about his family? About his trust fund?

Fuck. Had he just fallen for the biggest honey pot scam ever? If it was, the *goodbye and thanks for the memories* letter was an interesting ploy. But she could be playing the long game.

Thank Christ he'd worn condoms.

He shook his head. No. *Hell no.* Eleanor—*Nell*—had seemed too damn genuine. *He'd* approached *her* for God's sake. She'd have still been there trying to disappear inside that plant if he hadn't made the first move, he was sure of it.

God, was his radar for scheming women really that far off? It had taken a huge hit since Anna, but still…

He stood. He had to find her. Had to talk to her.

It took Bodie about fifteen minutes and one overheard conversation in the dining room to ascertain that Eleanor had left the building. She'd hightailed it back to *Shady Gums*, the Davis family cattle property, at five in the morning.

Were they the actions of a woman who was planning on using him as a meal ticket? He wouldn't have thought so.

But he still needed to talk to her.

He got the opportunity about half an hour later when he spotted one of Ryder's sisters heading to the buffet unattended. Liza? Lisa? He couldn't remember off the top of his head.

Damn it, if he'd remembered the names of his best friend's sisters a bit better, he wouldn't be in this predicament right now.

"Hey Lisa." He sidled up beside her, and she smiled in acknowledgement. So…Lisa it was.

"Hey Bodie, great game yesterday."

He nodded distractedly, wondering how to approach

the subject but knowing he had to be quick. He wasn't sure how long he'd have her alone in a crowded dining room full of people who all knew each other. "I was wondering if you could give me Nell's—" He stumbled over the name. She'd always be Eleanor to him. "Mobile number?"

Lisa stopped serving herself scrambled eggs, the spoon paused halfway between the plate and the buffet. She blinked at him, clearly startled by the proposition. "*You* want Nell's number?"

Ryder's sister was a pretty blonde, very attractive, but her obvious incredulity pissed Bodie off. Why he should feel so defensive and offended for Eleanor after she'd lied to him and ruthlessly slept with him, he didn't know. But he did.

"I was chatting with her last night about some Victorian stuff—"

Lisa interrupted with an eye roll. "Sorry about that. I hope she didn't bore you to death?"

Bodie stiffened. "Not at all." Still, she shot him a pitying smile. "I was telling her about this dress my family has in a First Fleet collection and she wanted to know the details, but I heard she's already left?"

"Ahh. *That* makes more sense."

Lisa resumed her activity like the world had suddenly been righted and life could continue. Like some old dress was the only reason a guy would be interested in her sister. But Eleanor was sweet and soft and passionate, and that made her ten times more attractive than her sister.

"Well, I'm not sure if she'll know what to do when she gets a call from a guy, but she does love an old frock."

Lisa quickly rattled the number off. Bodie tapped it directly into his phone, thanked her politely, then headed out the front door to call Eleanor in private.

He walked to the edge of the footpath as he called the number. Leaning his shoulder into one of the support poles for the overhead balcony, he glanced up and down the main street. It was deserted at this hour on a Sunday morning.

The phone rang and rang and he didn't think she was going to answer it when it clicked in his ear and he heard, "Hello?"

She sounded breathless and Bodie shut his eyes trying not to think about how breathless he'd made her last night. "Hello, *Nell*."

There was a long silence during which his heart thrummed like a rotor in his chest. He was pretty sure he could *hear* her brain clanking as it grappled with a solution to this clearly unexpected predicament.

"How did you get this number?" she finally asked.

"Lisa gave it to me."

"*Lisa?* You asked *Lisa* for my number?"

Her panic rang clear as a bell down the line. "It's okay. I made up some story about an old dress, a family heirloom. She bought it."

"You know, men in Victorian times weren't allowed to address women by their first names unless they were engaged."

Bodie may just have laughed at the nervous reply so similar to her nervous prattle of last night had the sick feeling in his gut not intensified. What did she mean, *engaged*? Was this where she laid her cards on the table? Where she tried to threaten or blackmail him?

"Are you proposing to me, *Miss Davis*?"

Her breath hitched in his ear and he liked it. "Look…I'm sorry, okay. I shouldn't have…"

No, she bloody well shouldn't have. Bodie went on the attack. "Why didn't you tell me?" He kept his voice low, but there was no mistaking the streak of grimness. "He's my *best friend*."

Silence hummed down the line between them. "Would

you have slept with me if you'd known?"

What the fuck? *Was she crazy?* "Did it seem like I had some reckless death wish to you?"

Another pause. "No. Which is why I didn't tell you."

Her husky voice filled his head and, despite everything, he wanted to be back in bed with her and to hell with the consequences. "Jesus, Eleanor." He pressed his forehead against the pole. "This is serious."

"Relax. I'm not going to tell Ryder. I'm not going to tell *anyone*. And I don't expect a declaration of undying love from you or a visit to my father for my hand in holy matrimony. I love my life out here just fine. I don't want any part of yours. Just notch me up as another one night stand—I'm sure you've had plenty of those—and go back to Sydney."

Considering how many one nighters he'd had since breaking with Anna last year, Bodie could hardly be affronted by her assumption, but last night had felt different.

And how the hell was he supposed to face Ryder again?

"Goodbye, Bodie. Thanks for last night. Have a nice life. Don't ring me again."

The line hung up in his ear and Bodie pulled his mobile away to look at it, stunned at the turn of events. If Eleanor Davis was after his money or looking to make trouble for him or the team, she wasn't being overt about it.

He relaxed, his faith in her *and* his radar restored even if the thought of never seeing her again, never *being* with her again, put a crazy kind of itch in his blood.

But if that's what she wanted? *Fine.* She was Ryder's sister for fuck's sake. It was just easier all round.

"Hey man."

Bodie tensed as Ryder clapped him on the shoulder right on top of the scratch marks his sister had left only hours before. He tried not to wince as a surge of guilt swamped him.

"Where the hell did you get to last night? You find someone to kiss your groin better?"

A spike of guilt stabbed Bodie in the side as he forced out a laugh. "Nah man, I was around."

Deny, deny, deny. That was his father's favourite catchphrase. Unless they catch you red-handed, son, it's your word against theirs. Deny. Bluff. Obfuscate.

His old man was such an asshole.

"You were too busy checking out your fiancée's ass most of the night to notice shit."

Ryder laughed. "She does have a spectacular ass."

Bodie nodded, trying and failing not to think about Eleanor's ass. Round and soft, the cheeks pale in the dark of the room.

Crap. He was *doomed.*

• • •

Bodie was beat. Sweat dripped off him after the gruelling training session. They may have won the city country match on Saturday, but Griffin King, their tough-ass coach, didn't let them rest on their laurels, especially as they were only halfway through the season. It was Monday and they were back at it.

He sagged onto the wooden bench separating two rows of lockers and reefed his shoes off, groaning as his arms ached. Griff had ridden him particularly hard today. It was almost as if the coach had known all about Bodie's monumental fuck up on Saturday night.

He wouldn't be surprised. Griff may have perfected the art of saying very little, but he seemed to see an awful lot. He hadn't been at the party because Griff *never* socialized, but somehow he just *knew* shit.

Bodie stretched out the traps on either side of his neck

as the clatter of cleats and the buzz of smack talk swirled all around him. He pulled off his sweat-soaked shirt. He needed a hot shower for his aching muscles. An ice pack for the whack he'd taken to his shoulder during training. And some ibuprofen for his niggling groin.

Although that was nothing to do with rugby and everything to do with the blueness of his balls and the number of hard-ons he'd suffered in the last forty-eight hours. Eleanor's sweet welcoming softness and her breathy noises of satisfaction had been playing on repeat and his whole groin area *ached* for more.

"Well hello, *hello* and what do we have here, gentleman?"

Bodie froze as Lincoln Quinn's voice from somewhere close behind brought him back to reality. "Spidey's found himself a hell-cat."

Fuck. He'd forgotten about the scratch marks.

"Dude? You holding out on us?"

Within seconds, he had a bunch of half-naked, sweaty jocks staring at his back and no comfortable way out of the situation.

Deny, deny, deny.

He was just going to have to put up with their crap and head to the shower as quickly as possible. And avoid Ryder's gaze altogether. Dexter Blake whistled appreciatively as he inspected them. "On the shoulder, too. That is some serious damage."

"Yeah man, your mother really goes off," Bodie deflected to much hilarity from everyone, including Dex.

"Never knew you had it in you," Tanner Stone, the team captain, said.

"Look a couple of days old to me," Linc mused.

Which Linc would of course know in his former role as team man-whore, before Em had tamed him.

"You *did* hook up in Bungindally, you dirty bastard,"

Ryder accused. "Didn't I tell you those country girls are wild? Spill, man."

Yeah. *Nah.* Not even if they held him down and all farted in his face. Bodie didn't think *I banged your baby sister five ways to Sunday* would go down so well with Ryder.

Hell, he couldn't even look at his best friend. He stood. "I need a shower."

There was a bunch of masculine jeers. "Hold the phone, boys," Tanner said, clearly amused. "It's serious."

Bodie's hackles rose, knowing it could never be anything more than one night because she was Ryder's sister and oh yeah, she'd *rejected* him. Right now, with every part of his body bitching at him, it was just another thing pissing him off.

"It's not what you think." He reached for a towel and slung it over his shoulder. It hadn't been a sleazy hook up. Eleanor had been different.

"Nah bro," Donovan Bane said as he crossed his thick, tribal tattooed arms across his huge chest and smiled cheerily. "You just cut yourself shaving, right?"

The guys hooted out some laughter and exchanged high fives as Bodie rolled his eyes. "Bite me." He slammed his locker door shut and pushed past the gathering.

"I think somebody already did," Ryder called after his disappearing back.

Without breaking stride, Bodie flipped them the bird. Their good-natured laughter followed him all the way to the showers.

And that was pretty much how it went for Bodie for two and a half months. Life went on, the ribbing and the questions eventually died down about the mystery woman who'd scratched up his back, and he could look Ryder in the eye now without a spontaneous surge of guilt. But he hadn't been able to get Eleanor and their night together out of his head.

He knew it was impossible to go there. For a start, she lived a twelve-hour drive away, although that was no real hurdle. It was two and a half hours by plane. The bigger issue was she hadn't wanted any more to do with him and he *couldn't.*

Because Ryder.

But he thought about her often, not even consciously most of the time. She was just there when he was at training or playing a game or at the regular poker night with the guys. God alone knew how many times he'd been to her business webpage just to see what she was up to.

She ran a blog through the site which revolved around her dress projects. He'd read every blog entry and looked repeatedly at every piece she'd ever made for her customers. He was probably the most well-informed elite rugby player in Australia on the difference between a flounce and a *bouillonne.*

The most interesting pieces, though, were lingerie. Very old-fashioned. How something that covered so much could be so damn sexy, he didn't know.

It just was.

That find had led to several hours down internet rabbit holes as he *researched* the subject, ending up on a site that specialised in Victorian pornography. Which, in turn, had given his night time fantasies—of which there had been many—an erotic edge. Eleanor running around in pantaloons and him calling her *Miss Davis* as he bent her over a chaise, taking full advantage of the open crotch seam.

It had been agony. But he'd accepted that was just the way things were between them—a one-time thing that could never be anything more. Until he received a text out of the blue…

Am in Sydney for five days. Can we meet?

Bodie blinked at the screen. He hadn't quite believed his eyes when her name had come up and his hand shook—actually shook—as he opened the text. The substance wasn't exactly stimulating, but what had he expected?

A titty pic? From someone who made frilly neck-to-knee *undergarments*?

She'd made contact—that was all he cared about, even though he shouldn't. For a moment, he even let his imagination go to all the places he'd been wanting to go with her since he'd last seen her two and half months ago.

Eleanor. *Ryder's sister.*

His fingers gripped the phone harder as he reread the text, his initial *hell yeah* tempered slightly.

Why was she here? What did she want?

He wasn't worried about her intentions. He'd long dropped any, admittedly lukewarm, suspicions he'd had of her. He *was* worried she might be as horny for him as he was for her. What if she'd figured they were in the same city so why not see if he was up for a little fun?

Christ… He almost went blind letting that little scenario play out for long delicious moments. It made sense. Why else would she be looking him up? *But.* Nothing had really changed. She was still his best friend's sister and he couldn't go there again.

Once could be forgiven. He hadn't known who she was and he could put his hand on his heart and plead ignorance. But twice?

That was a *deliberate* action.

Still, he couldn't deny the strong urge to see her again. He hadn't got to say a goodbye last time so maybe it could be a kind of closure for him. He could take her out for coffee. Or a meal. To a movie if she wanted. They could do that. Indulge in adult conversation over some kind of beverage then say goodbye.

Yeah. They could do that.

Would like that very much, Miss Davis. Where. When?

His finger hesitated over the send button. He wasn't trying to flirt by using Miss Davis. He was just trying to keep it light between them. Surely after a night in bed with her they were allowed to tease each other?

Fuck it. He hit send. And waited.

Not for long as it turned out, his phone chiming less than a minute later.

Tonight. Six? I'm at the Four Seasons. Darling Harbour. Room 922.

Tonight? *In her hotel room.* Not down at the hotel bar or at a nearby restaurant, or any of the bajillion *highly populated* venues in that area? He swallowed.

Bodie had his regular boy's night poker game at seven but he could call in and see Eleanor first. In fact, it would give him an excuse not to linger. In her room. With a bed.

Fuck. He swallowed again. Was he strong enough? Did he trust that his loyalty to Ryder and the team couldn't be tested by a woman he'd been fantasizing about in Victorian lingerie for the last two months? Christ…

Why don't I meet you in the bar at 6?

He sent that without thinking twice—sent it before his libido could hijack his common sense and he ended up in her room, with a bed. The reply was just as rapid-fire as the last.

Can't. Friend arriving at 6.30. Need to get ready.

Okay. So that made sense. Women were, after all, masters of multi-tasking, and if she was on a strict timeline—as was he—then it meant there wouldn't be any time or focus on other things.

OK. See you then.

He hit send, his pulse drumming forcefully through his veins, anticipation sitting rock-like in his stomach. In a few short hours, he'd be seeing Eleanor again. All he had to do was remember he was a mature, twenty-six-year-old man, not a fifteen-year-old horn dog.

And if that failed, chanting Ryder's name over and over should do it.

Chapter Five

Eleanor almost threw up while she waited for the knock on her door. Considering she was eight weeks pregnant and hadn't thrown up once, that was saying a lot about the internal ruckus currently tying everything in knots.

Breathe, Eleanor.

She dragged air deep into her lungs, held it for three seconds, then let it out again.

She knew what she had to do. Open the door. Invite him in. Tell him she was pregnant. Assure him she didn't want anything from him, that he could be as involved or uninvolved as he liked. Answer any questions. Make another date to talk it over more fully. Then send him out the door before Miriam arrived to help her dress for the function.

Absolutely do not, under any circumstances, flirt with him, touch him, kiss him.

This wasn't about *hooking up* again even if she was so damn desperate for it she'd probably hump his leg the second she opened the door. She thanked God she'd suppressed the urge to make an appointment at the hotel beauty salon for a spot of vagazzling. She needed *all* the barriers in place to stop herself from dragging him into her room and having her way with him.

Not that a wild and woolly...*frontier* had stopped her—*or him*—last time.

She *had* to remember why she'd called this meeting in the first place. She'd contemplated not saying anything to Bodie until after the first trimester. When the risk of miscarriage lessened. But this *Studies in Victoriana* symposium she was attending for the next five days had gifted her time in Sydney, and therefore the perfect opportunity to broach the subject with Bodie.

She didn't know how he'd feel or what he'd do or say, but she'd kept the pregnancy to herself for a over a month now and it didn't seem right to keep it from him any longer. Deception didn't sit well with Eleanor.

Lying by omission to Bodie that night in Bungindally had been hard enough, she had no wish to do it again.

And he was going to need some time to get used to the news. She'd had a month to adjust to the situation. It was only fair that he have some time to come to grips with what would, no doubt, be a bit of a bombshell.

They had, after all, used condoms.

A knock startled her, and Eleanor's hands found her stomach, trying to draw strength from the fledging life growing inside her. She was suddenly unsure about *everything*. About the way she felt about him. About the wiseness of this course of action. About the trackie daks and T-shirt she'd pulled on after her shower to try and appear as sexless as possible.

A second knock and a flash of déjà vu from that night in Bungindally hit her, and Eleanor quickly crossed the room to open the door before the third knock, and she slipped them both back into that night of utter debauchery.

Right. As if...

She was wearing the daggiest clothes in her wardrobe, her hair was caught up in a huge plastic claw at the back of her head, and her pubes were going to need a machete to hack through them.

He was a sexy, elite rugby god and she was a…bloody country bumpkin.

Eleanor squared her shoulders. *Just get it over with.*

She opened the door abruptly, her heart careening crazily in her chest as their gazes locked. He was even more beautiful than she remembered and she almost whimpered out loud as an avalanche of lust-soaked pregnancy hormones almost buried her self-control.

Do not touch. Do not touch. Do not touch.

He towered over her, his hair wet as if he'd just come from the shower but not feathery and flyaway like hers. No, his was damp and gorgeously rumpled. His shoulders stretched out a T-shirt better than any shoulders had a right to and his jeans stretched across quads better than any man had a right to *possess.* His tanned, muscled arms, his throat and his face with its perfectly symmetrical three-day growth were achingly familiar and he was wearing the same aftershave he'd worn that night, drenching her in headily sexual memories.

Do not touch. Do not touch. Do not touch.

A lazy half smile followed by that funny little half bow he'd performed that night in the beer garden, and she was a goner. "Nice to see you again, Miss Davis."

Eleanor's resistance snapped so loudly, she'd bet her last cent it registered on a Richter scale in California somewhere.

She touched. Hell, she *grabbed.*

Her breath rushed out in a *whoosh* as her hands clutched at his waist, then his chest, then his shoulders as she pushed up onto her tippy toes and climbed him like a tree. His big hands on the back of her thighs urged her up, and they parted to accommodate his hips.

She wasn't sure if she kissed him or he kissed her, just that their lips met and she was moaning and he was groaning and all the worry and doubts and denial these past couple of months fell away as she fed on his mouth.

"*Fuck.*"

Her lips vibrated with his guttural profanity as he stepped into the room, kicked the door shut, and pressed her against it, his body flush with hers, his big hands hot on the juncture where her ass met her thighs.

"Jesus, Eleanor." He was panting as he wrenched his mouth from hers. "I can't be doing this." But then his mouth slid to her neck, his teeth scraping along the mad flutter of her pulse.

"I know." She angled her neck to give him more access, her heartbeat roaring in her head like a waterfall, her breath squalling like a hurricane in her lungs.

And she did know. *Neither* of them should be doing this. She at least needed to tell him about the baby first. But her body, starved of him—*of his touch*—for so long, was powerless to resist. It was like he'd opened a whole new world to her a couple of months ago, given her the briefest glimpse of paradise, then taken it away again.

But he was back and he'd kissed her and he'd opened the door again and she wanted—no, she *needed*—to rip the bloody thing off the hinges. Although some of that could probably be attributed to those pregnancy hormones.

The sudden grinding of her hips into his certainly was.

"I've just…" She broke off, rubbing herself against him again. She moaned as liquid heat pooled behind her belly button and between her legs. He felt so good. *So hard.* "I've missed you so much."

He let out a strangled kind of oath and then he was kissing her again, knocking her head back against the door with a *thunk* she barely registered, thrusting his tongue in and out of her mouth, doing with it what she wanted him to be doing with his *cock*.

She'd been practicing that word, trying it on for a while now, and she *liked* it.

He groaned again and pulled away, shaking his head as if to shake off the intoxicating pull of her. "We really should stop."

It might have sounded more convincing had his mouth not been all wet and red from their kisses and his cock hard as stone between them.

"Yes." Her head was spinning, her breathing tatty and wild, and she wanted to mewl in disappointment. "Right." But she didn't make a move to get down.

"Ryder."

She nodded again. "Yes." He didn't have to say any more. To explain. She understood that being here like this put Bodie in a very awkward position. That he wasn't comfortable *having relations* with his best friend's sister behind his back.

But he didn't let her go. He didn't put her down. Just stood there between her legs, her ankles locked around his ass.

And God almighty…he was in a perfect position as far as she was concerned, all his hardness jammed against the juncture of her legs, where everything was swollen and achy. All she needed was a little friction.

A little movement to make things better.

Her hips—or maybe it was her hormones—decided to take control, flexing along the length of him, his hardness meeting her softness. Her eyes fluttered shut and her whole lower half shuddered in ecstasy.

He was staring at her when she opened them, his hands gripping and ungripping the backs of her thighs, a battle of devils and angels going on behind his suddenly hooded eyes. The rough serration of his breathing was like a physical caress.

"Christ," he muttered, the surge of lust heating the inky blue of his gaze to indigo, shaking his head like he couldn't wrap his head around what was happening. "I want you too much."

He slammed his lips down on hers. And he didn't let up. He kissed her like he was *starving* and she knew exactly how he felt, returning his hunger—sating it. Her senses were full of him, the sound of his breath, the taste of his mouth, the intoxicating essence of him invading her sinuses until he was inside her head.

Her hips bucked wildly, *uncontrollably* against him. She could no more have stopped them seeking pleasure than she could have flown to the moon. Her body was so primed for gratification—for *him*—it was seeking it of its own volition and she was too much in thrall to leash it.

She'd have never thought it possible that a person could orgasm through two sets of clothes from a bit of bump and grind but she was *so damn close*. And she needed him to be inside her when she came.

She *craved* it.

"Bodie." She broke off, gasping for breath as she reached between them. "I need you in me."

"No."

His denial was swift and his mouth was back on hers, but he clearly had no intention of leaving her hanging as a hand left the back of her thigh and pushed inside her underwear. Eleanor gasped, her head falling back as Bodie's fingers quickly slid into the slickness there, one sliding deep inside her, the other finding the erect little pearl between her legs.

Eleanor flung her arms around his shoulders, pulling him close as a wave of pleasure like a contraction rolled from her belly button to her knees. "Yes," she cried out, riding the glide of his fingers shamelessly.

He didn't speak, just buried his face in her neck, grinding his hips against her from the outside as his fingers worked her from the inside, setting up a relentless pace, destroying any sense of reality, any thought of consequence.

It was just him and the loud suck of his breath and his fingers. Rubbing and working. His breathing getting lower and rougher and deeper. Pushing her closer and closer until she came.

Quick. And hard. And loud.

Too much anticipation, too much abstinence, too many nights of fantasising about Bodie. It rose up and out like a volcano, exploding from the point where his fingers were jammed inside her. She went rigid for a moment before turning molten, waves of pleasure undulating, drowning her in bliss and bathing her in light, incandescent and sweet as she chased the fading tail, leaving her heavy and languid and boneless.

At some stage, he removed his hand from her underpants and Eleanor moaned as excruciatingly sensitized tissues shuddered at the stimulus. She blinked, coming back to herself, desperately gathering all the far-flung pieces of her sanity and trying to cobble them together.

Slowly, he eased her down and her hands slid from around his shoulders. He waited for a beat or two after her bare feet hit the floor before he took a step back, but Eleanor still clutched the door, sagging against it for support as her legs wobbled.

God alone knew what she looked like.

She felt like she'd been thrown into the eye of a storm and tossed out the other side. And Bodie looked like it. He certainly wasn't the sleek pro-rugby player who'd been standing at her door. He'd definitely suffered a little storm damage despite the tension in his body.

He was still strung pretty taut.

And why wouldn't he be? She'd gotten off, not him, and he looked like he needed it in the worst kind of way. A twinge of feminine possession sizzled in the slick folds of her sex and, legs stronger, she took a step toward him.

"No." He held his arms out to ward her off. "Just you." His voice was husky but there was no mistaking the authority as he took another step back.

Eleanor's fingers curled into her palms, a trickle of disappointment hitting her system. "You don't want to…?" She dropped her gaze to the thick bulge testing the confines of his fly.

Because she really, really did and it must really, really *hurt.*

"No." He shook his head, but the sizzle lighting those indigo eyes matched the sizzle between her legs.

"Ryder?" It was a rhetorical statement, but he gave a grim nod as he shoved his hands on his hips. "I'm seeing him tomorrow, but you *have* to know I won't say anything to him, Bodie."

He gave a harsh half laugh. "Yeah, well, I'm seeing him in half an hour. I've got to look at your brother across a poker table tonight and pretend that I didn't just finger fuck his sister against a hotel door."

It had been two and a half months since she'd heard Bodie swear, and it hadn't lost any of its impact. Her nostrils flared at the deliberate profanity.

Why was his filthy mouth such a turn on?

She was sophisticated, for crying out loud. She read *Austen.* Jane, who was exceptionally clever with words, had never stooped to using such common vulgarities in her life. She didn't need *F* words. Eleanor should be *scandalized.* Instead, she was wondering how much more sexy Mr Darcy might have been had he not been quite so much a gentleman.

"Christ." He raked a hand through his hair. "There's a

special hell for guys like me, you know? Guys who have sex with their best friend's sister."

"Well technically...we didn't actually have sex this time, so..."

"You think Ryder's going to think that *fingering* you to orgasm is a lesser sin?"

Eleanor's belly twinged again at his language. Man, he was *good* with those *F* words.

The bedside phone jangled into the silence. *Ack!* That'd probably be Miriam, checking she was still on target.

"Look...I'm sorry, but I have a friend arriving in—" She checked her watch. "Fifteen minutes."

Warmth stole across her cheeks. Gracious! From the time she'd opened the door until now—which included a pretty spectacular orgasm—had been fifteen minutes.

He'd made her come in a paltry few minutes.

"So." He shoved his hands on his hips. "You just wanted to *hook up* then? Or was there some other reason you lured me here?"

Hmmm. He was pissed at her. His tone was light but his jaw was tight and she hadn't missed his emphasis. Well, he could get in line, she was pissed at herself as well. But, as someone who'd only ever *hooked up* once, she refused to be embarrassed by it.

She was wearing that sucker like a banner of honour.

Except she didn't have time for his snit now. In retrospect, it had been naive—although she preferred to look at it as hopeful—to think she could even raise such an issue on such a strict timeline. Particularly in a hotel room. With a bed.

Not that they'd used the bed.

But she'd wanted their conversation to be private. She thought she at least owed him that. A moot point when they hadn't actually gotten around to discussing it, though. If she'd chosen a bar or a coffee shop she'd have *told* him at least.

Instead of ending up debauched against her hotel door.

Lesson learned. *Only be around Bodie in a crowd.*

"I do want to…catch up," she confirmed, because she was too chicken to say *tell you you're going to be a baby daddy*. It was hardly fair to drop that then send him on his way, was it? And she sure as hell wasn't going to tell him about the baby while he was self-flagellating over their little indiscretion just now. Especially not with her friend's imminent arrival.

"This thing tonight runs to nine and you're out, too, so why don't I ring you tomorrow and we can organize a time to meet?"

He regarded her for long moments. How he managed to dominate the room so effortlessly she had no idea. But he did. Standing there all tall and brooding, six foot to her five, his hands on his hips. For a crazy beat that seemed to slow time and thicken the air, she thought he was going to close the distance and kiss her again.

But it passed.

"I'll be at training all morning. Try me after one."

Then he stalked past her, the door clicking shut as he left the room.

• • •

Bodie was playing terrible poker. Which had everything to do with sitting here in Ryder's apartment, the memory of his sister's keening cry as she came trapped inside his head, the aroma of her clinging to his skin.

Juliet, Ryder's fiancée, was with the other WAGs and Val, the coach's daughter, at Dex and Harper's tonight—ostensibly for a girl's night but mostly to coo over baby Gemma who had been born a month ago. Not that her absence had been noted particularly by Bodie. Recriminations were rattling so loudly around his head he could barely even hear the pound of the surf on nearby Coogee beach.

Linc looked up from his cards and said, "You know what this poker game needs?"

"More pizza," Donovan said as he scavenged through the empty boxes looking for another slice and finding none. The half-Maori man-mountain was always hungry.

The usual answer to Linc's question was *chicks*. Although with four out of the six of them—including Linc—now spoken for, he said it more out of nostalgia than anything else.

Which was just as well—Em would kick his ass.

"Seriously though." Linc looked at each of his happily-involved team mates, appealing to them all individually. "We need to spread the love. Get Spidey and Dono hooked up."

Donovan shook his head in disgust and glanced at Bodie in solidarity. "Only one thing worse than a reformed smoker, and that's a reformed man-whore."

Bodie couldn't agree more. "He's like frickin Cupid."

"Yeah." Donovan nodded. "A big, blond, naked baby."

Everyone laughed, including Linc, who ploughed on regardless of the insults, obviously warming to the topic. "Dude." Linc took a swig of his beer as he lanced Dono with a look. "I've seen what you're packing downstairs. The ladies have *got* to want them some of that."

"I have a kid." Donovan had been married once a long time ago and his teenage daughter lived with her mother in Auckland. Considering the distance and the gruelling demands of his rugby schedule, he was incredibly involved in her life. "She's my focus."

For a man of few words, people took notice when he spoke. *Nothing to see here, move along.* Four sets of eyes shifted to Bodie and Dono grinned.

Five, actually, if he counted the rheumy gaze of Ryder's pathetic looking, long-haired Chihuahua, Mona. The pink ribbon tied around her neck in no way counteracted the ugliness of that one fraggle tooth. She'd been sitting there watching him all night, her head turning from side to side as if she knew what Bodie had been up to with her master's sister.

The damn dog was *judging* him.

He glared at Mona and she promptly peed on the floor. "Your dog wizzed."

"Jeez, man." Ryder rose from the table. "She's sensitive. Don't frighten her like that."

He grabbed the kitchen towel they'd been using as napkins, picked Mona up, murmuring low assurances as he kissed her head and wiped at the small puddle before resuming his seat with Mona firmly ensconced on his lap.

Tanner laughed first, followed by Dex, then the rest of them. Big bad country boy Ryder Davis and his girly-ass dog.

"Fuck you all," he said, calmly picking up his cards and asking Dex, who was dealing, for three.

"Em's got some cute teacher friends," Linc suggested and any hope that Bodie had that the subject had been dropped died a quick death. "Although I will deny I ever said that if any you bastards pass that on."

More laughter. "She has a friend called Karen, she's a little on the prim side but…"

"Nah man," Dex interrupted, "Spidey likes his women with claws, remember?" It was the first poker night Dex has attended since the baby had been born, and he was clearly enjoying getting back into the swing of things.

Bodie tensed, raising his gaze over the top of his cards to meet Mona's stare. The dog was giving him the evil eye.

"I bet some of those drag queens at *The Cock and Bull* could scratch your back up good," Tanner suggested. "And enjoy doing it."

The club, in Sydney's infamous King's Cross, was part owned by Ryder, and the drag show there was second to none, but Bodie couldn't even *look* at his best friend right now. Christ, if he didn't think it would cause more questions he'd get up and leave.

"Jesus, for a bunch of dudes who are all loved up, you seem to be a little too interested in my sex life. Aren't you all getting enough without living vicariously?"

Linc laughed. "*Vicariously.* Listen to Spidey and all his big private school words."

Bodie threw his hand into the discard pile. They were crap. They'd been crap all night. He was in a crappy mood, and Linc's shitty juvenile prattle, which usually made him laugh, was getting on his last nerve. Not even a royal flush at this moment could have improved his mood.

"I'll have five more," he said, his jaw ground tight.

The guys exchanged looks around the table. Tanner tisked. "I think your problem is you haven't been using the five you got." He partially curled the fingers on his left hand and made a wanking motion.

Ryder laughed. "Nah. He just needs another country girl, is all."

Bodie could feel his cheeks growing warm and was grateful for his three-day growth. He didn't need another country girl.

Just one. Just Eleanor.

Who'd come all over his hand in a breathtakingly short amount of time a few hours ago.

"I'll ask Lisa next time I'm talking to her, she'll know someone up for a good time."

Fuck-a-doodle-do. Bodie's temper was fraying at a rate of knots. Would this never end? "Why not just pump Eleanor for some names when you see her tomorrow?" he snapped.

Jesus. That *would* be the ultimate irony.

Ryder blinked. "Nell's coming to town?"

Bodie froze—shit…he was pissed off, and he had her on the brain and it had just slipped out.

"Wait..." He frowned. "How do you know my sister's going to be in town?"

Yeah, *dufus*... How *do* you know jack shit about Ryder's sister and her movements? *Crap.* But surely the bigger question was *why didn't Ryder know*? Eleanor had told him she was seeing her brother tomorrow, and Bodie had assumed Ryder knew not only that she was coming to town but she was, in fact, *in* town *right now*.

Driving him crazy.

Bodie hoped he didn't appear as startled as he felt while his brain quickly flipped through suitable answers, because he didn't think telling Ryder he'd just made *Nell* come her brains out against her hotel door would be well received.

"I...bumped into her in the city...this afternoon." Christ... Could that have been any more lame?

"Wait." An even bigger frown cracked Ryder's face. "How do you know my sister?" Mona stared at him through rheumy eyes and bared her fraggle tooth. Yeah, *dude,* explain that one.

Deny, deny, deny.

"We met at your engagement party." Part of the bluff, according to his old man, was to ground it in as much truth as possible.

"Oh. Right..." Ryder, clearly satisfied with that, grabbed for his phone. "She must have come down for some costume expedition or something. She usually lets me know, though." He scrolled with his thumb for a moment or two. "She hasn't texted me."

Bodie couldn't confirm or deny why Eleanor was in town, except perhaps to fuck with him. They hadn't got around to chit chat. "Maybe she was surprising you?" She'd sure as shit surprised him.

The urge to explain and apologise for jumping the gun about his sister's presence in the city rode Bodie hard but he ignored it. The less he said, the less that could be used against him in court.

Yeah… He'd been raised by the antichrist.

"Well anyway." Linc clapped him on the back. "Problem solved mate, there's your country girl."

His deliberate needling of Ryder worked a treat and Linc laughed at Ryder's death stare. "Even if she wasn't my sister and completely off limits to you filthy bastards"—he gave Bodie and Dono the evil eye in turn—"she's one country girl who wouldn't be giving it up for your pretty three-day growth. Amongst her many…*quirky* attributes, Nell announced at Christmas dinner at the age of eleven that she, like the Virgin Mary, was saving herself for *the one*."

Bodie blinked. *What. The. Fuck.*

"Yeah but, how old is she now?" Dex asked. "I wanted to be Luke Skywalker when I was eleven."

"She's twenty-six. And last time I teased her about it a few months ago, she proudly told me she still had her V card."

"Sure, man," Dono quipped, "so's my mumma."

Everyone laughed. Everyone except Bodie. Because things were falling into place. *Holy fuck*. Eleanor was a *virgin? Had* been a virgin?

With a sinking feeling worse than losing a grand final, Bodie knew it was true. It made sense now. Her tightness, the heady mix of her eagerness and shyness, that moment she made him wait after he'd pushed inside her.

Christ. He should have guessed. Why hadn't he guessed?

"So what, she's saving herself for…God?" Tanner asked.

Ryder shook his head. "Mr Darcy, I think."

More laughter. Bodie swallowed. Great. She'd been waiting for Mr fucking Darcy and he'd given her some sleazy hotel hook up. She'd been waiting for the gentleman, and he'd given her the cad.

He was going to hell. And *that* was too good for him.

Chapter Six

Bodie almost knocked Eleanor's hotel door down an hour later. How he'd sat through the game as long as he had, he didn't know. His brain had been turning in circles, his actions operating on some kind of autopilot—crap autopilot, considering how much money he'd lost, but somehow he'd managed to give the appearance of playing cards.

The door remained stubbornly closed and he muttered, "Come on, damn it," under his breath as he belted it again.

He didn't really see Eleanor standing there through the red mist of his anger. God alone knew what his blood pressure was right at the moment. "You were a virgin?" he demanded. She blinked, then blushed, but he was too pissed at himself *and* her to care.

She sucked in a breath. "Why don't you say it a little louder, so the rooms down near the lifts can hear it too?"

She stepped back from the door, and Bodie stalked inside, straight to the large window. "Imagine my surprise," he said, looking out over the twinkling lights of Darling Harbour as his heart hammered in his chest, "when Ryder tells me all about his sweet virginal sister Nell who's supposedly saving herself for *the one*."

"And my state of virginity was being discussed at your poker game because?"

The mist thickened. "It came up," he snapped.

Bodie took a few deep breaths designed to settle the hard edge of his anger and dissipate the swirling red mist cloaking him in irrationality.

It didn't help.

He whipped around to find her standing calmly just behind him. Her hair, swept up into some fancy, decorative creation, left her neck and shoulders bare, which was distracting as hell.

Jesus Christ, he wasn't here to ogle her.

He folded his arms and glared at her. "I didn't know."

She quirked an eyebrow. "How were you supposed to know? We don't tattoo it to our foreheads, you know. Or do you expect some kind of blood bath on the sheets from your virgins?"

Bodie's jaw clenched at her flippancy, ignoring her implication that he was some kind of man-whore. Up until a year ago he'd been a one-woman man. "You should have told me."

Just like she should have told him about being Ryder's sister. She'd hidden a fuck ton of stuff from him that night.

"You want to give it back?"

A blood vessel throbbed dangerously at Bodie's temple. "If I fucking could, *yes*."

She sighed, her shoulders lifting, her chest expanding, which dragged his gaze lower. To her cleavage, all soft and bouncy and pushed up in gorgeous offering like it had been that night, and he remembered how desperately he'd wanted to dive in.

The same kind of desperation assailed him now as he

took in the flouncy, ruffled floor-length dress with the tiny waist that could easily have been at home in the pages of a history book.

"What would you have done differently?" she demanded.

Bodie pulled his gaze up from all her softness with difficulty. Her fiery whiskey eyes were flashing. "I don't know, Eleanor, but maybe I might have gone slower, taken my time a bit. Asked if you were okay. Or whatever the fuck it is a guy's supposed to ask a woman during her first time. Maybe I might have even taken all my bloody clothes off."

She folded her arms, and his gaze was drawn again to the sweet swells of her cleavage. "For the record, I was fine. I have absolutely no complaints."

The throb of anger was morphing into an entirely different throb now as that night came back to him, and she watched him all soft and sweet and round and tiny-waisted telling him she had *absolutely no complaints.*

The sweet pulse of desire slithered through his veins. He ignored it. *He hadn't come here for this.*

"I...should have known." He shoved a hand through his hair, denying the gnaw of need whispering through his flesh. "You were so shy, so...tight but I just assumed..."

She raised both eyebrows at him this time. "Assumed?"

"I don't know." He shrugged. "That you did...Pilates or Bikram yoga?"

"Bikram yoga?" She laughed, exposing the vulnerable line of her throat and, in his mind's eye, he could see himself muzzling her there. "In Bungindally?"

He groaned. "Look, I don't know, I just..."

She stood before him, clearly waiting for him to complete his sentence, but how could he concentrate on his virgin rage when she was all soft and pushed up and bouncy like that and her bed was sitting in his peripheral vision all white and beckoning?

"You what?"

"I...*Christ*." He shook his head, his distraction complete. "What are you wearing?"

She blinked, then glanced down her body before returning her gaze to his face. "It's a Victorian-era dress based on a pattern from the eighteen-fifties. I made it."

It didn't really help. Because all he could wonder about was what else she might have made for it? Like, maybe some of that Victorian underwear he'd seen on her site? Corsets and petticoats and pantaloons. *Crotchless* pantaloons.

What was she wearing *under* all that fabric?

He swallowed. "You're very talented."

"Thank you." She shook her head dismissively at the compliment.

"I mean it." Bodie wanted her to know he was impressed. "I've...visited your website. I know how many hours goes into something like that." He nodded at the dress, his pulse spiking as he wondered just how quickly he could get her *out* of the damn thing.

"Really?" She seemed taken aback by the admission. "You've been to my website?"

"Often."

Bodie supposed he shouldn't give so much of himself away. His father wouldn't approve a bit, but the interest in her gaze, the *delight* in the way she smiled at him, made him pleased to have opened up. A new throb roared to life in his chest.

"And does the rugby guru have a favourite frock?"

Bodie chuckled. He wasn't sure how they'd gone from her withholding vital information from him to frocks. Or from rage to desire for that matter, but the atmosphere fairly hummed with it.

"I'm more a fan of the ummm...undergarments." And now he was flirting.

She smiled. "I bet you are." She was flirting, too.

His pulse rate picked up again, not racing but thudding harder in anticipation, desire buzzing like electricity through his system with every contraction of his heart.

This was not good. It was crazy. It wasn't enough that he'd made her come against the door four hours ago, he wanted more. He wanted her again.

He couldn't seem to get enough of her.

And if the sudden husky burr to her breathing was anything to go by, he wasn't the only one feeling it.

Crap. He *really* hadn't come here for this.

"I should probably go."

He stepped away from the window, making a beeline for the door, passing between her and the bed, but then she stepped into his path and he halted. He was suddenly grateful for the closeness of the bed as every bone in his body seemed to dissolve.

Except for the one in his pants. It was like granite.

"The problem with these frocks," she said, taking a step closer to him, "is how difficult they are to get in and out of without help."

Bodie swallowed as his gaze dropped to the soft bounce of her cleavage. "Yes… That would be a problem." Bodie assumed that her friend had helped her get into the thing.

She shrugged and took another step. "I can do it, of course, but it's much easier with another person."

"Right."

Their gazes locked and held for long moments before she turned her back to him. "Do you think you could help me with these buttons before you go?"

The aroma of orange blossoms filled his nostrils as Bodie's gaze snagged on her hair. It, too, was done in the kind of style he'd seen in history books. The fine chocolatey strands styled into a mass of soft ringlets. A handful of dainty flowers pinned and tucked amidst the curls seemed decorative but Bodie thought they might actually be keeping the whole thing together. A couple of strands of hair had either fallen down to tease her neck or had been deliberately pulled to do so.

Either way, it made him want to press a kiss to her nape. Maybe even nip it a little.

"Bodie?"

Her uncertain, husky voice broke into his reverie and he glanced at what looked like a hundred buttons starting at the notch of her spine that divided nape from back and ending below the waist. His fingers itched to touch them.

"I don't suppose I can just undo the top one and rip?"

It was a joke, but his fingers tingled to do just that, and he was very much afraid that he might be tempted to follow through if she didn't specifically tell him not to.

Rip her dress open like she'd done to his shirt in Bungindally. Follow the dictates of a body demanding he go all Incredible fucking Hulk.

She laughed and it was soft and low and rough, cupping his aching balls in a velvet hand, reminding him that while she'd gotten off a few hours ago, he had not.

"It took me a day to make and sew on all those buttons and their loops."

So, that was a no then.

Bodie took a steadying breath and slid his fingers to the top button. He fumbled it immediately, his fingers feeling too big and clumsy for the delicate work. Give him a football and his hands were sure and steady, but a row of fabric-covered buttons…?

Fine motor skills had never been his forte.

He took another breath, stooped a little closer, and tried again. This time he successfully freed the slippery button made from the same fabric as the dress from its delicate lacy loop. One down, about a hundred to go.

If the slow reveal didn't cause him to stroke out…

Within ten buttons he was starting to see skin, and he stopped counting as his body tuned into other things. Like the uneven pitch of her breathing and how his breath disturbed the tendrils of hair that had escaped from her do and the goose bumps feathering her skin.

And her big-ass bed one step to his left.

The silence grew and stretched around them. Who'd have thought the brush of fingertips against fabric could sound so loud? Or air escaping from lungs could tumble out like a hurricane then be cut off like a garrotte at the discovery of a snowy white corset.

More buttons revealed lace and boning and the hourglass curve of waist and hip and it took all Bodie's willpower to keep to the task and not to stray. There was something to be said for modesty and a slow reveal, and Bodie was never going to underestimate the power of the tease ever again.

It was the most delicious kind of torture, touching her like this—methodically, impersonally. When all he wanted to do was let his hands wander, explore, discover.

He popped the last button. "Finished." His voice was like gravel, his dick like stone, his balls so damn heavy they were practically dragging on the ground.

"Thank you."

He barely had time to register the gratifying unsteadiness of her voice before she shrugged her shoulders, pulling each puffed sleeve down her arm and off completely, removing the dress to the waist and revealing the corset almost in its entirety.

Despite the fact he couldn't see much of it from here, blood rushed to his cock. Where it was going to go he had no idea—there was no room at the inn down there, it was already as tight and full as humanly possible.

"Can you undo the petticoat tie?" Another husky request.

Bodie glanced down to find some kind of plain cream garment cutting off the view of the corset from the waist down, tied at the back with a pink ribbon. He slid his fingers onto the simple bow and rubbed the fabric between his fingers.

"This pink ribbon?"

Bodie needed to be sure. Who knew there so many damn working parts to this kind of get up? Although he was all for undoing all the ribbons and all the buttons and whatever else he could. He eyed the back of the corset—how did *that* come undone?

"Yes."

Bodie, his lungs feeling too tight for his chest, pulled one of the tails and the bow slid undone, the fabric of the petticoat loosening immediately from Eleanor's waist.

"Thank you," she said again, then, as he watched, she pushed the dress and petticoat down in one movement until it pooled around her on the floor.

She stepped out of the circle of fabric and pushed it out of the way with her foot, turning to face him. She was in nothing but a corset and a pair of pantaloons. Her breasts were pushed up and almost spilled out of the corset completely, her waist nipped in to form a perfect hourglass, the bottom of the corset dipping down to form a peak between her hips. The pantaloons were short, not long, coming to mid thigh and puffy around the hips. With rows of lacy ruffles on the ass.

Goddamn, sexy as fuck, *ruffles.*

Jesus. How had men of that era ever got anything done knowing their woman was somewhere in that get up?

If she'd leaned in and stabbed him he couldn't have been any more stunned. "Bloody hell," he whispered, staring at her, not able to stop.

More blood diverted and Bodie groped for the bed beside

him as he became light-headed. A stupid idea, considering his eyes were now level with those sexy pantaloons. He fisted his hands in the bedcovers to stop himself from reaching for her.

"So..." He cleared his throat because gawping at her like an idiot was starting to get old. "This is the kind of... underwear they'd have worn back then?"

It was the first thing he could think of instead of something lewd and un-Mr Darcy-like such as *let's fuck* but still, he couldn't believe he was talking about two-hundred-year-old fashion with a raging twenty-first-century boner.

"No." She shook her head slowly as if she couldn't believe he was talking about it either. "The corset isn't a proper one, there are hooks and eyes at the back. But I didn't have time to get into the proper one with the laces earlier."

Bodie almost forgot that he was the reason she hadn't had time as the thought of a lace up corset cavorted in his head like a burlesque dancer.

"And they would have worn a chemise under the corset to keep it off the skin, but we tend to wash more frequently than they did, so I usually give that a miss. They probably wouldn't have worn these short pantaloons either underneath such a formal dress but nobody at the function knows what's on under your skirts, and I've just made them and wanted to try them out."

Bodie swallowed, thrilled that *he* knew what was under her skirts. "I'm pleased you did." He stared at them, their lack of sheerness exciting as hell. Knowing what was under them but not being able to see, forced to use his memory, his imagination, cranked his anticipation to a loud screech.

"You like?" Her voice was quiet, her cheeks pinking up, her gaze not quite reaching his.

Eleanor Davis was a conundrum. She stood boldly before him in her underwear after requesting he help her unbutton, yet her blushes were never far from the surface and she could barely meet his eyes at the moment.

"Oh…I *like*. In fact, I think you should wear *only* them at all times in my company." He smiled, trying to tease her out of her shyness.

"Oh really?"

"Are they…"

God, it was completely inappropriate to ask what he wanted to ask. This was Ryder's sister, for fuck's sake. But considering what he'd already done to her—on two separate occasions—this was tame. And he *needed* to know.

He cleared his throat again. "Crotchless?"

She didn't say anything for long moments, her gaze locking with his, the fiery whiskey hue sparking and flaring as if she was fighting the same kind of battle he was. Finally she moved, stepping closer. One pace. Two. Stopping in front of him, her knees putting pressure on his to open.

Bodie couldn't have stopped them from admitting her had his life depended upon it. He eased his thighs apart and she stepped forward until she was right between his legs and he was forced to fall back on his elbows or do something completely *ungentlemanly* and bury his face in her pantaloons.

Another long pause as if she was trying to gather her courage, her chest rising and falling in a wonderfully agitated rhythm that shifted her cleavage in a breathtakingly sexy way. Bodie salivated as he thought about running his tongue along the soft swells pillowing from the snowy white corset.

Slowly, she slid her left knee over his thigh until it was anchored on the mattress, parting her legs. The smell of orange blossom and musk invaded his senses.

"Why don't you find out?"

Her voice was husky and tremulous, and even though Bodie could see it had taken all her bravado to be so fucking bold, she didn't break eye contact.

Whatever valid reasons there were for him getting the hell out of this room and running as far away from Eleanor Davis as possible—and there were many—they all meant squat in this moment. He slid his hand onto her left thigh as he slowly levered himself up into a sitting position.

She shivered and her skin puckered into goose flesh beneath his touch as their gazes locked. Slowly his hand moved higher, traversing the fabric hiding her from his view. His heart punched hard against his rib cage and her breathing roughened as his hand trekked closer and closer to her inner thigh, finding the seam before brushing higher and higher.

A groan slipped from Bodie's throat as he found the opening of the fabric, gaping wide, begging to be taken advantage off. Christ, he could smell her, an intoxicating mix of old-fashioned citrus and aroused woman and his whole body tightened.

"Tell me to leave," he whispered, his gaze clinging to hers.

He'd go, if she asked him.

But she shook her head slowly, her hand sliding to his shoulder, the slight dig of her nails reminding him of how good they were together. "Stay."

He drew in a ragged breath, their gazes still locked as his hand breeched the opening of her pantaloons and found the seam of her sex. Her eyes widened and her breath hitched, and Bodie's heart just about burst through his chest at the heat of her.

"*Fuck*." He groaned as her slickness coated his fingers. "You're wet."

He pushed them inside her then and she gasped, grabbing his shoulder as her eyes closed and two sets of nails dug into his shoulders and he wanted her just like that always, her breathy moans driving him crazy, ecstasy etched on her face.

"Why can't I get enough of you?" His voice was low and

gravelly.

It should be enough that she was Ryder's sister but it wasn't.

Her eyes opened, pinning him with their intensity, the spill of her cleavage rising and falling in utter hypnotic glory. "I don't know."

Bodie didn't have any time to analyse her comment before she was sliding her other leg over his thigh and leaning down, and he was stretching up, muttering, "You are a vixen," against her mouth and then they were kissing deep and wet and long.

Then somehow she was straddling him, that damn gape in her crotch lining up perfectly and her moans were in his head and citrus was invading every breath he took and his heart was tripping and air was sawing in and out of his lungs as his hands roamed over the hard cage of the corset, hungry to feel every inch.

Her hands were between them, plucking at his belt and unzipping his fly and pulling his aching cock out of his underwear and guiding it between her legs and he thanked *Jesus and all the sweet, sweet angels* for crotchless nineteenth-century underwear as the head of his cock slid through the wet heat of her sex.

She moaned, and all he could think about was being inside her, deep inside, all the way to the hilt, making her pant and cry and *scream his name.*

Nothing but her and her pleasure and all her tight, slick heat driving him on as he slid inside her.

He groaned at the perfection of the moment and kissed her, swallowing her cry as he entered her. Swallowing her whimpers and her moans as his big hands spanned the waist of her corset, using the hourglass curve to his advantage, lifting her off and thrusting her back down on his cock—*hard.* Wrenching out of the kiss to watch the bounce of her beautiful cleavage, the light blue veins mesmerizing as her breasts threatened to spill out.

She whimpered with every withdrawal and cried out with each thrust and quickly, so quickly she was clutching convulsively at his shoulders and shaking and trembling and her wild noises swelled like a rock concert in his head until she gasped and jerked to a halt and finally bellowed his name.

Bodie muffled her ecstasy with his mouth as she shuddered in his arms, clamping tight around him, pushing him higher and higher until he was shuddering too, deep, *deep* inside her, his heart pounding, his head pounding, his fucking *toes* pounding as he wrung every last ounce of pleasure out of it for both of them before collapsing back against the bed gasping and sated, Eleanor sprawled on top of him.

Fuck!

He felt like he'd been sucked into a whirlwind, spun around a thousand times and twirled out the other side. His head was spinning. God knew he'd been mauled on the field plenty but never so thoroughly as this. Who knew a five-foot-nothing chick could be more effective than a hulking line backer?

And, *yet again*, he was still fully dressed.

"It seems like getting you off with all my clothes on is going to be our thing."

Warm air tickled his neck as she belly laughed, and he almost groaned out loud as the shift of her abdominal muscles had a *very* intimate ripple effect.

Christ! He shut his eyes as he realized he was bareback inside her. *He hadn't even thought about a condom.*

He *always* thought about a condom. He was either totally fucked or utterly, hopelessly bewitched. Maybe both.

"This is probably not the best time to raise this." His hand slid to her back, the bones and furrows of the corset sexy as fuck beneath his palm. "But I didn't even think about a condom."

Chapter Seven

Eleanor was ripped out of her post-coital bliss by the roots of her hair. It had been nice drifting along there, his cock still full inside her, everything stretched deliciously, the low buzz of her orgasm still sizzling along nerve endings, the furtive knowledge that it could be roused again lying latent in every cell.

This was her in. To tell him the truth. About the baby. And hope like hell he wasn't too mad about it *or* the fact that she'd chosen to seduce him—*twice*—in the last few hours without telling him first.

It was going to be a hell of a buzzkill.

Reluctantly, she rolled off him, her breath hitching as he slid free of her, a very gratifying groan of protest sliding from his lips. She sat, shuffling to the end of the mattress, her feet flat on the floor, conscious of his big frame stretched out behind her, the bulk of his thighs in her peripheral vision.

"Eleanor?"

His hand landed on the small of her back. She felt its warmth even through the thick fabric of the corset and she soaked in the comfort of it. "I like that you call me Eleanor."

She was obfuscating but the truth was, after her bombshell, he might never call her *anything* ever again. There was some rustling behind her, the sound of a zip and then the mattress dipped and he was upright, his arm brushing hers.

"You're freaking out about the condom?"

If only.

Surprisingly it wasn't the pregnancy bit she was having problems with. It was the deception of not telling him about it straight up.

Getting all…*jiggy* with him *twice* before telling him.

"If you're worried, don't be." The note of caring in his murmur almost undid her and, absurdly, Eleanor wanted to cry. "I can assure you, I'm clean. Until a year ago, I was in a long-term relationship and while I did go a little crazy for a while after the break up I *always* wore a condom. Of course, there is the matter of pregnancy—"

Eleanor snorted, cutting him off, staring at her hands, grabbing one with the other to still the tremble. It was a most inelegant noise—Queen Victoria would not have been amused.

"That's not an issue."

"You're on the pill?"

"No. Just can't get any more pregnant than I am."

He went very, *very* still. "You're…pregnant?"

"Yes."

"And I'm the—"

"Yes." She cut him off, quashing the quick spurt of outrage she'd felt at the question. It was fair enough. They'd had one night together, they'd used protection, and she hadn't seen him for ten weeks.

Just because she'd been a virgin before didn't mean she hadn't been with every man in Bungindally since. *Clearly* he'd woken some kind of dormant nymphomania if the last few hours were any indication.

There was a long pause. “But I wore condoms.”

“I know.” But she doubted they were the first people it had ever happened to. Eleanor finally dared to look at him. The bronzed planes of his face had paled a shade or two and a deep frown crinkled his usually smooth forehead. She needed him to know that she wouldn’t lie about something like this.

That when it came to the paternity of the baby growing inside her, there was no doubt.

“I’ve only ever been with you.”

He nodded slowly, and she could see the dawning of belief in his twilight eyes. “Okay.” His calmness was soothing. She hoped his lack of yelling and calling her names was a good sign.

He rose from the bed and headed for the window, his back to her as he stared at the view. He shoved his hand through his hair, the action squeezing her heart. She didn’t know what he was thinking or feeling and it made her nervous but she took a deep steadying breath and waited.

He was trying to process something that she’d already processed. She was going to have to cool her heels for a bit.

“Why didn’t you…tell me sooner?” He turned to face her, his hair deliciously rumpled.

“I’m sorry.” She stared at her hands. “I planned to tell you this afternoon and then we…”

“No, I mean…why didn’t you tell me when you first found out?”

“Oh.” She glanced at him. He didn’t seem pissed off about the delay, just curious. “Well…I’m only eight weeks. If I hadn’t been coming to Sydney, I probably wouldn’t have said anything until I was twelve weeks, after the first trimester. Twenty percent of pregnancies end in miscarriage and the highest risk window is the first twelve weeks, so…”

A look of alarm stiffened his features. "Shit. Did I… should we have been…" He shoved another hand through his hair. "Christ, I was banging around in there like I was drilling for fucking oil."

Eleanor laughed at the analogy, and some of the tension left her shoulders. "It's fine. Normal sexual activity—"

She stumbled over the words. She couldn't believe she was saying them in front of a man that she'd just had *normal sexual activity* with—*twice.*

She'd had *relations* with Bodie Webb. Sydney Smoke elite. Sporting royalty. Rugby hottie.

Sex god.

"Is allowed," she continued. She'd Googled it.

He nodded, the tension across his shoulder visibly easing. "Thank you. For telling me."

"Of course." She frowned. "I had to. It's your baby, too."

"Are you…okay? Have you been sick or…?"

A spot right in the centre of Eleanor's chest warmed. She'd just told him he was going to be a father and he hadn't sworn or yelled or accused her of lying or being some kind of…jezebel. He'd obviously been shocked, but he was calm and concerned about her well-being.

No wonder her brother liked him so much.

She stood because she wanted him to know she wasn't some delicate creature that required TLC. She'd been brought up on a cattle station and, like all country people, she'd soldier on.

His gaze zeroed in on the soft pillows of her cleavage and even though it was highly inappropriate during this very serious conversation she couldn't stop the low tug of desire.

"I've been fine."

He raised his eyes and shoved his hands into the pockets at the front of his jeans. "No vomiting at all? That's good."

Eleanor shrugged. "Some mild nausea from time to time.

I'm just usually regular as clockwork and when my period didn't come and my boobs felt sore…"

His gaze dropped to her *boobs* and the tug became a yank. Yeah, she probably shouldn't have mentioned them, but how could she want to go *again*?

Sure, she was new to this sex thing, and she'd read enough books and seen enough TV to know that *some* men and women couldn't keep their hands off each other. She'd bet her last cent Lizzie had kept Mr Darcy in bed for a week after their nuptials.

But nothing had prepared her for the hot lick of lust turning *her* into some kind of *wanton*.

"Should you be wearing that thing?" He lifted his gaze from her corset to her face. "Aren't they too restrictive or something?"

Eleanor, trying to drag her mind off a body that was *apparently* no longer under her control, looked at the garment, running her hands down the bodice as she so often did, leaving them flat against the boning low on her stomach. "It's more the lace up ones that are restrictive."

Although hell, if he wanted her to take the damn thing off she would. The suggestion hovered on the tip of her tongue but fortunately he chose that moment to step toward her and the words died before they got to her lips.

"Could I…?" He gestured toward her middle with a vague wave of his hand.

Eleanor's hands flattened a little more on her stomach. Did he want to…feel the baby? A sudden surge of shyness hit her at the intimacy of the action. "I'm only eight weeks, there's nothing to feel."

"I know."

But his eyes were glued to where her hands were splayed, and she could no more have denied him than played in the Smoke front row. "Okay, sure…" She dropped her hands. "If you want."

He was with her in three strides, one arm sliding around her shoulder, tucking her in close to his side as the other hand slid onto the place where hers had been. There was no way he'd be able to feel even the shape of her belly through the fabric, but his touch, the sentiment, made her heart flutter.

The silence stretched as they stood in a shared moment, and it seemed like the most natural thing in the world to lay her head against his arm. She shut her eyes and imagined how nice it would be to have him by her side like this for the entire pregnancy, his hands reaching for her swelling belly at every opportunity.

"We should get married."

Eleanor's eyes flew open. She lifted her head from his arm and looked at him, gaping. The tempo of her heart picked up until she was sure he must be able to hear it. "*What?*"

Was he serious?

"You're pregnant. With my baby. *I'm* the father. It's the right thing to do."

"If we were living in the nineteenth century, maybe."

She gathered all her willpower and pulled away from him, pacing to the window as he had done twice tonight, uncaring who might be able to see her in her corset and pantaloons. She turned to face him, giving whatever random strangers might be down there a view of her ruffled ass.

"I thought you adored all things nineteenth century?"

"I adore the *fashion*. Not the lack of female agency."

"You're my best friend's sister, and you're pregnant with my baby."

"So you want to get married because you think Ryder, who *by the way* has absolutely no say over my life, will bring out his shotgun?"

He shook his head. "I want to marry you because it's the right thing to do."

It was hard to try and make rational arguments when Bodie was making all the ones that her hopelessly romantic soul craved. How many historical romance novels had she read just like this? An honourable man doing the *right thing*—the responsible thing—fulfilling his duty to the woman he'd deflowered then *got with child*.

And falling in love with her.

But this was the twenty-first century.

She'd done a lot of Googling since their night in Bungindally. Bodie Webb was a sporting celebrity from a wealthy family. He could have anyone. How long would it take before the restrictions of a wife and a child that he took on out of a sense of *duty and responsibility and honour* would start to chafe?

And what about love?

"Maybe in Jane Austen's day, Bodie, but not now. Nobody gets married these days because of a pregnancy—"

"Yes they do," he interrupted.

She conceded his point with a nod. "And we have a divorce rate over fifty percent." He conceded hers with an answering nod. "All I'm saying is, we don't need to rush into anything. Society's not going to disown me. We have options."

"Well, you've obviously given it some thought?" He shoved his hands on his hips, a stubborn set to his jaw.

Eleanor had been giving the situation a *lot* of thought these past weeks—there'd been little else going on inside her brain—but none of the scenarios had involved Bodie wanting to be overly involved, let alone her husband.

She hadn't even dared let her mind—or her *heart*—go down that path.

"I thought I'd raise the baby on the farm. It's a great place for a kid to grow up."

The inky blue of his eyes turned bleak. "And what about me? What I want?"

"Of course you could have access."

"Define *access?*"

"I don't know… I guess we'd have to discuss that." She took a step toward him but he stiffened and she stayed put. He was only a few meters away but he was so distant he might as well have been in the middle of the harbour. "I'm sorry, Bodie. I just didn't think you'd want to be overly involved."

"*Why* wouldn't I want to be involved in my kid's life?" he demanded.

Eleanor blinked at the harsh edge to his voice. "Because I know how hard you guys work to get to where you are and stay there. Playing at such an elite level, the game becomes your whole life and distractions can be harmful to your career. I've grown up with Ryder, so I understand probably better than most."

He visibly relaxed as she spoke, the white at the angle of his jaw disappearing, the tension in his neck and shoulders dissolving.

"Your work, your *life* is here in Sydney. And, well…let's face it…we were just a one night stand with consequences. I don't expect you to disrupt your whole life for me."

She was trying to be sensible and practical. And fair. She wanted to be *reasonable.* Give Bodie an out. She wasn't stupid enough to buy into some knee-jerk happily ever after with him.

"I wouldn't think less of you because of it."

He covered the distance between them, a hand sliding onto her face, cupping her jaw. "*I'd* think less of me." He dropped his head and kissed her, soft and sweet, and her body leaped to the call of his.

He pulled away, his gaze fixed on hers, his lips wet. "I don't want a scenario where I live here and you live there and I see my kid at the end of every footy season."

The pad of his thumb stroked lazily along her cheekbone,

and Eleanor fought the urge to shut her eyes.

"I watch Donovan do that, and even though he knows it's the most stable thing for his kid, it kills him every time his daughter gets on a plane and heads back to New Zealand. I want to be able to kiss my kid goodnight, *every* night."

The passion and intensity in his gaze and his voice slid into her heart like a stiletto. She didn't want to deny him, she just couldn't wrap her head around his easy acceptance of it.

"I thought this would be a bombshell," she whispered.

He gave her a half smile. "It is."

"A *bad* bombshell."

He shrugged. "It's done. All that remains is how we fix it. So…what do you say? Wanna get hitched?"

Eleanor blinked. Ever since she picked up her first Georgette Heyer at the age of eleven, she had been dreaming of this moment. The moment a man asked her to marry him.

It was a far cry from the romantic idyll she'd pictured. But then she hadn't been twenty-six and *knocked up* in her fantasies either. She knew it was stupid in the circumstances to mourn the death of a silly childhood dream but a pang of loss caused a cramp in the centre of her chest anyway.

Not that it meant she was resigned to this fate, though.

The decision to marry shouldn't be a snap one, particularly when the groom was a virtual stranger. "Bodie…" She slid her hand onto his palm and gently eased it off. "We hardly know each other. This is…too much."

In twenty minutes, he'd yelled at her for being a virgin, *fucked* her for being an evil temptress, and proposed to her for being pregnant.

Her head was spinning, even if his wasn't.

"Right, yes…of course." He nodded, very businesslike all of a sudden as he stepped away from her a safe distance. "You need time to think. You're here for five days, you said?"

Eleanor blinked at the rapid change. "Yes. I'm heading

home on Monday. But I'm not sure I'll be ready to—"

He held up his hand to silence her, and she obliged. "Just promise me you'll think about it?"

Was he crazy? How was she going to think about *anything* else? "As long as you promise me *you'll* think about it."

He gave her a grudging smile, a little bit sheepish and a lot sexy. "Deal."

He looked like a guy who was holding all the cards. Every inch the decisive rugby player weighing her up for any weaknesses just before he mowed her flat. His gaze dropped to her pantaloons and made its way slowly over the corset, his smile fading.

Maybe he didn't hold *all* of them.

"I'm leaving now. While I still can." His hungry gaze took another tour of her body and goose bumps flared from her shins all the way up to her scalp and she wanted him again. But she could hardly reject his proposal of marriage then ask him to stay.

"I'm going to ring you in a couple of days—" He held up his hands as she opened her mouth to object. "Just to check in. But if you need anything in the meantime...*anything...* Buttons undone. Petticoats untied. A completely, no-strings-attached, no-need-for-reciprocation-orgasm *or two—*" Bodie grinned. "Call me. I'm your guy."

Eleanor choked out a laugh. She'd forgotten with the baby and the sex and the out-of-the-blue marriage proposal how fun he'd been that night in Bungindally. How they'd laughed into the night. "My hero."

He grinned. "They don't call me Spidey just because I look hot in a Lycra suit."

He left then and Eleanor threw herself down on the bed, suddenly wobbly-kneed and light-headed. It was madness to be grinning like a loon, considering her predicament.

But she was.

• • •

Bodie knew he shouldn't feel so happy about the pregnancy, but he couldn't help it. If any other woman had landed a baby daddy bombshell on him, he would have freaked out.

Hell, he *should* be freaking out regardless.

As Eleanor had said—distractions could be deadly to a career in elite sport. But he wasn't.

His outlook on life had been kind of dark since breaking up with his ex. He'd lost faith in the order of things—in being rewarded for good and working hard and doing right. Cynicism had started to infect his thoughts and his actions.

Rugby, his team, had been the one bright light in it all.

But now there was Eleanor. And his baby.

He'd hardly slept a wink all night thinking about it, and he was paying for it today as Griff put the Smoke through his usual punishing training regime. But Bodie didn't care how much his body ached, he felt like fucking *Spider-Man*.

Sure, he wouldn't have *chosen* this particular hurdle at this time of his life. But he refused to see the baby as any kind of burden. Being an only child, he'd always wanted kids—a whole tribe of them—and Eleanor's calmness had been the prism he'd needed to see that it could work out.

It made him feel guilty for his initial reaction, though, and he was infinitely pleased she hadn't been looking at him when she'd told him. Years of being Conrad Webb's son had taken their toll. Growing up in an environment where everyone's motives were suspected was a lot of baggage to overcome, and he was ashamed to admit his first thoughts had been to wonder if Eleanor had planned it all along.

To trap him for his money. Or his fame. Or whatever.

But he'd dismissed the dark whispers as they'd formed in his head and her *I've only ever been with you* had clutched a big handful of his gut and squeezed. They'd used condoms, she'd tried to absolve him of responsibility, *and* she'd rejected his marriage proposal.

If Eleanor Davis was some gold digger after his trust fund, then she was *really* bad at it.

The truth was, he was going to be a father and she was the mother of his child. A vision of Eleanor, a baby suckling at her breast, hit him square between the eyes and almost brought him to his knees.

A football to his solar plexus actually did.

"*Spidey,*" Griff barked. "What the fuck is your problem today?"

Bodie smiled despite not being able to fully catch his breath. "Sorry, Coach." He rubbed his chest. "Distracted."

Thinking about being a daddy.

"We don't pay you to be distracted." Griff glared at him, hands on his hips. "Go and run that shit off. Come back when you're ready to concentrate on rugby."

He pointed to the track circling the outside of the footy oval and Bodie, breath regained, hit it without protest. It didn't matter. He could run around it all day. He was going to be a *daddy*.

He was fucking indestructible.

His father, who hadn't yet forgiven him for breaking it off with Anna, was *probably* going to have a stroke. Ryder, who *probably* wouldn't *ever* forgive him for sleeping with his sister, was *definitely* going to kill him. And when he was done, Ryder's father and probably every other man in outer woop woop would no doubt send out some kind of posse to string him up to the nearest tree.

But he was going to prove them all wrong. And marrying Eleanor was step one.

Bodie had surprised even himself last night by blurting out the proposal, but once it was done it had made absolute sense and he'd gone for it. He'd learned from the best about acquisitions and mergers—strike while the iron was hot. Don't give your opponent time to regroup.

Fortunately, Eleanor had reminded him she wasn't a string of numbers on a spreadsheet. She wasn't a piece of property or a tasty blue-chip stock and he'd snapped the fuck out of it, but it didn't mean he'd given up.

If his father had taught him anything, it was to go after what you wanted. And rugby had taught him not to wait for it to come to you.

Chapter Eight

Eleanor checked the bedside clock as her phone rang at six the following night. Expecting it to be Miriam confirming the time for the fashion parade, she snatched it up without checking.

"I have a proposal."

Not Miriam. *Not even close.*

Eleanor gripped the handle. Was she always going to melt a little when she heard Bodie's voice or was it just a new thing? A novelty. She hoped so. Otherwise she was going to spend a lot of her life like a marshmallow on a stick over a roaring hot fire—gooey in the middle one moment, bursting into flames the next.

"Another one?"

She had to play this cool, show him she wasn't going to be bullied or railroaded, no matter how much her breath hitched at the word *proposal.*

God, was it only twenty-four hours since he'd first come to her hotel room last night? So much had happened in such a short space of time.

He chuckled low in her ear, and it sent shivers skating across her skin. She sat on the bed as her knees threatened to give out. "Don't go home on Monday. Move into my apartment with me, Miss Davis."

Eleanor's pulse fluttered madly. "Bodie."

How dare he? Did he know how tempting it was to use such a formal address? *Yeah*. He totally did.

"No, wait…hear me out."

Hear him out? His low, sexy *Miss Davis* was giving her ear an orgasm. She'd sit and listen to the man recite the bloody phone book.

"I can apply for a notice of intended marriage tomorrow after training at the registry office in the city, and thirty days later we can be married."

Thirty days. In thirty days, she could be Mrs. Bodie Webb. Her head spun. This was crazy. She *couldn't* marry him.

"But…we don't know each other."

"So…come and live with me for thirty days. Let's get to know each other. And then at the end, if you think you can stand looking at my face every morning, we can go down to the registry office and make it official."

Eleanor quashed the well of disappointment at the thought of a quickie marriage at City Hall. No heart-thumping courtship, no romantic proposal, no asking her father for her hand in marriage, no Victorian-inspired wedding dress she'd always dreamed of making for herself, no local church with her nearest and dearest as witnesses.

No I love yous.

Even women in Victorian times who found themselves in the family way out of wedlock had a proper, if somewhat hastily arranged, wedding.

"C'mon, Eleanor. Let me show you how it can work, how good we could be together."

Eleanor had no doubt they'd be very good together. But being together for a month with them both on their best behaviour and a *lot* of sexy times wasn't exactly a courtship.

"I'm not talking about sex. It'll all be completely above-board. You can have the spare room."

Eleanor blinked. *Did he mean tha*t? "You…don't want to have sex?"

She'd tried to keep the incredulity out of her voice but it had crept on in anyway. *Really?* Just sitting here talking on the phone with him, his voice all low in her ear, was making her wet.

"Christ, Eleanor." His laughed sounded more than a little strangled. "I want to have sex with you on every surface in every position in every room of my apartment. I want it to be so plastered with our DNA, my whole place will glow like a fucking Christmas tree under one of those black lights those forensic dudes use. I want you to come so loud so often the neighbours will always be calling the cops on us. And I want to fuck you so bad right now my cock is about to go all Incredible Hulk on me and bust right through my jeans."

He paused and she heard the ragged tempo of his breath despite the ragged tempo of her own. After twenty-six years of no sex, Bodie had just waved nirvana in front of her face.

"But I won't," he continued, "if you don't want to. Because I need you to know getting married isn't just about a steady supply of sex for me."

Eleanor couldn't speak for a beat or two. She could barely see straight, let alone form a coherent thought. "And if I wanted to? With the…you know…black light thing?"

"I am at your service."

She didn't need to see him to know his lips had curved into a wicked smile. It was present in the rich lilt of his voice.

I am at your service.

Eleanor knew words. She'd read a lot of them. She knew

they could amuse, infuriate, inspire. *Titillate*. But she didn't know until right now they could reach inside underwear and insert themselves inside vaginas.

His wicked smile arced from the phone into a wicked whisper inside her head—or maybe it was coming from areas a little further south. Why not do something outrageously reckless for once? Why not finish what she'd put in motion when she'd slept with Bodie in Bungindally? Why not go the whole hog and do something completely and utterly irrational?

Completely unpredictable. Completely freeing.

Why not shack up with a guy for a month and have so much sex she'd never quite walk the same way ever again? People back home already thought she was kooky. What was one more oddity to add to the mix? One more thing for them to gossip about?

Bodie was right, they couldn't have a marriage based on sex alone. Not when a child was in the mix. But how would she know if they were at all compatible with her in Bungindally and him in Sydney?

"Eleanor?" The rough burr of his breathing stroked the shell of her ear. "Say yes."

"I…" She wasn't sure when she was going to be capable of anything more.

His laughter stroked her nipples to tight points. "You need a moment."

A moment? She needed a slug of whiskey and a vibrator.

"Okay, Miss Davis." His voice buzzed over her skin. "How about this? I'll ring you on Sunday and ask you again. Give you some time to think about it, okay?"

She somehow managed a squeaky, "Okay."

"Have you got some function you're going to tonight?"

Eleanor blinked to clear the sexual fog from her brain. He wanted to talk about *normal* things now? "Ah…yes. A

Victorian-era fashion parade. A couple of my gowns are being shown."

"More pantaloons?"

She smiled at the wry amusement in his voice. "There could be. It's unladylike to talk about such things to a gentleman, however."

Not quite as unladylike as exposing them to his view, or straddling his lap whilst wearing them.

"Is that a fact?"

Eleanor put on her best prim-and-proper voice. "It is."

"But I'm not a gentleman."

"Then it's definitely inappropriate." His laugh told her he was completely unconcerned, and she squeezed her thighs together tight. "What about you, what are you up to tonight?" It seemed only polite to ask, given he'd shown interest in her activities.

"I'm thinking of hitting the shower after this."

Of course he was. She shut her eyes to stop the images but it was too late. Her brain already had him naked, water running over his torso. Running *lower.*

"You're already thinking about me naked, aren't you?"

Eleanor's eyes blinked open. "Absolutely not."

"Liar." He chuckled, and it was like honey over gravel. "You know what I'm going to do in there?"

His voice was a dirty whisper inside her head. "Get clean?"

"Oh no, baby. I'm going to get very, *very* dirty. You want to know how?"

"No." But it was the saddest, weakest, most reluctant *no* that had ever been spoken in the history of the world.

"I'm going to stroke my cock and think of you. You want to hear more?"

"No." Okay… *That* was the saddest.

Another gravelly chuckle told her he didn't believe her

for a second. "I'm going to imagine you in front of that big picture window in your hotel room, your hands up high on the glass, your gorgeous soft breasts—have I told you how much I love your breasts?—bouncing in that corset, your back arched, your ruffled ass—*God, those ruffles*—presented to me, and all of Darling Harbour watching as I fuck you."

She could just hear the saw of his breathing over the thud of her heartbeat and something else—the slow metallic give of a zipper…

Her breath roughened to match his. "Are you—" She stopped abruptly and blushed. *Do not ask him that.* She *couldn't* ask him *that.*

"Am I masturbating?"

Eleanor's heart lurched in her chest. The word had always sounded ugly and furtive to her but he clearly wasn't ashamed. He made it sound natural.

Hell, he made it sound like a *noble art.*

"Yes," he said, no hesitance, no embarrassment in his deep definitive voice. Just pure male pride.

Sure, babe, I got my cock in my hand, what about it?

"I couldn't wait for the shower. Is that okay?"

Okay? *Gracious.* Her heart tripped at the question. It shouldn't be. It felt like it should be…*illegal.* But an ache had taken up residence between her legs. "Yes."

His groan was like sandpaper in her ear. "I'm so fucking hot for you."

Her skin erupted into a million goose bumps, her nipples rubbing painfully against the inside of her bra. She shut her eyes and imagined his hand wrapped around his erection.

"Do you—" She faltered, blushing at the audacity of her question.

"Do I what?"

His husky prompt spurred her on to boldness. "Go fast or slow?"

"Slow." The words came out on another groan, sounding slurred, like he was on some kind of high, like he was drugged. "I want it to last but I'm so fucking turned on, so close to spilling my load."

His rough pants filled her head. "I'd like to see that."

Hearing Bodie masturbate was exciting enough. What would it be like to watch him commit such a…private act? Everything south of her belly buttoned tightened.

The ache became a throb.

"*Fuck*. Hold on." There was rustling in her ear. "I switched to FaceTime, look at your screen."

Eleanor's lungs felt too small for her chest. *FaceTime?* She hadn't even *thought* about that. About the possibility of *actually* watching him masturbate.

A gush of slickness between her legs joined the throb.

Slowly, she pulled the phone from her ear and changed to FaceTime. An image of him filled her screen, his features frozen in a rictus somewhere between bliss and rapture. His lips were parted and the noises slipping from his mouth were like hot tongues against her skin.

"Show me," she whispered. Her voice sounded foreign, but she didn't care. She was greedy for the sight of him.

For this risqué new thrill.

He lowered the phone, angling it toward his erection, and Eleanor stopped breathing altogether. She'd never seen anything more *male* in her life than Bodie Webb touching himself, and she thanked every shooting star she'd ever wished upon for phones with cameras.

It was breathtaking. His cock stood proud and taut. His hand gripped hard. The knuckles of his fingers were white. The thick spongy dome of the head was blushed a dark purple. The bead of liquid pearling at the slit was clear, almost glistening in the light shining down from above.

His hand moved like treacle. Up and down. Slowly. So

slowly. Like he was in some kind of thrall. His hips pushed up into each downward movement, dragging a groan from his throat.

It was poetry in motion and her sex clenched in response.

"You're beautiful," she whispered.

He groaned. "And you're sexy as fuck."

She let his guttural compliment go to her head. "It's so… tight." And he was squeezing so hard. "Does it hurt?"

"Hurts so *fucking* good."

"What would make it better?" She barely recognised her own voice.

He grunted. "Your mouth."

Eleanor's mouth flooded with saliva and her eyes widened as the imagery seemed to turn him on as much as her, his fist moving faster now, his thumb swiping over the head with every upward flex of his wrist.

"On your—" She swallowed. "Cock?"

"Fuck yes," he whispered, as his hand moved faster.

A surge of power swept through Eleanor's body, knowing in a way she'd never known before that she was in charge here. That she was turning him on with her words alone. Her breath hitched as she morphed into a woman she didn't recognise.

Someone daring. Someone who knew their way around a man's anatomy.

"Sucking it?" She crossed her legs as the throb between them became a screaming demand. "You want me to suck it?"

"*Yes.*"

The noises from his throat were low and keening now, his hand almost a blur. The camera wobbled and shook but she could still see the action. Her pulse thrummed in time to the beat of his hand. "I've never done that before. Will you show me, Bodie?"

"God...Damn...*Fuuuck.*"

Suddenly liberated, she pushed him more. "I'd like you to teach me, Bodie." Adrenaline at her boldness tripped her heart rate into hyper-drive. "I want yours to be the first... cock in my mouth."

He cried out. "Eleanor!" His hips jerked to a halt. And then he was thrusting again, shuddering, the camera unsteady as his cock rammed back and forth through the tight clamp of his hand.

She gasped at the first stream of white fluid spurted from the plump, flushed head.

"*Bodie.*" More slickness added to the wet heat between her legs and her mouth filled with saliva as she watched his hand wring every last drop.

She desperately wanted to be there with him. To have her mouth where his hand was, to make him come with her mouth as he had made her come with his. To taste him as he had tasted her.

She didn't know whether she'd like it or not. Two out of her three sisters were fans. Lisa said it tasted like warm curdled yoghurt with a toxic dash of bleach.

But she knew she sure as hell wanted to try.

They were both breathing hard as Bodie's hand slowed then stopped and still she couldn't drag her eyes off his erection. Even spent it was proud and firm.

He lifted the phone to his face, a satisfied smile relaxing his features. "Told you I wasn't a gentleman," he said, his voice still a little unsteady. "Sweet dreams."

The screen suddenly went blank and Eleanor flopped back against the mattress, her mind officially blown by the sweetest, sexiest, *dirtiest* thing she'd ever seen.

Seemed she wasn't much of a lady either...

• • •

Eleanor wasn't sure what time Bodie was planning on ringing her, but after a sleepless night Sunday dawned bright and clear and she'd made up her mind. Time to declare herself before she chickened out completely.

His phone rang for a long time and she almost hung up. Almost decided it was a sign she should heed. "Eleanor?"

The hot spike of adrenaline settled as did her madly tripping heart. He sounded sleepy, like she'd woken him, and she glanced at the clock. *Six.* It was late for her, being a country girl, but she'd thought he'd be heading to Henley stadium for training by now.

"I'm sorry, I woke you."

"I'm not." She could hear the smile in his husky morning voice. "What are you wearing?"

Eleanor blushed. Even just roused from sleep he had a way with words, his hushed tone somehow sexier. Deadlier. She wondered what *he* was wearing. She'd bet her Heyer collection he slept naked. She rolled onto her side and shoved a fist between her legs as things stirred to life down there.

"Don't you have training to be getting to?"

He laughed but it turned into a yawn, big and deep, and the sound undulated through the muscles of her belly. How on earth could a yawn sound so sexy?

"Our game's tonight."

"Oh, of course." Ryder had mentioned it when she'd seen him and Juliet told her he could get her tickets if she wanted. She'd had to decline because of the Albert and Victoria soiree on tonight.

"So…what *did* Victorians wear to bed?" he asked.

"That very much depended on your station in life and your views on modesty."

"They're pretty broad."

Eleanor smiled at the understatement, her brain flicking to the peep show he'd gifted her, but she continued doggedly on. "Mostly plain, thin, linen shifts in the early part of the century that became more decorative and flattering toward the end with the advent of the first commercial sewing machines."

"I love it when you talk dirty."

"Commercial sewing machines are dirty?"

"Sure they are. Talk sewing machines to me, baby."

"Bodie." She laughed. He was incorrigible.

"You're sexy when you get all scholarly."

And he was sexy *all* the time. She bet he even woke up sexy with sparkly minty breath and his hair perfectly coiffed. Her hair usually looked like a bird's nest that had been hit by lightning. "I'm trying to be serious."

His low chuckle tickled her ear, but when it petered out he cleared his throat and said, "Okay, okay, *serious*." He lowered his voice to sound like a serious television journalist. "So…I'm thinking that my preference between early and later examples of Victorian sleepwear would definitely lean toward earlier."

"I'd have thought your preferences would lean toward red, lacy, and teeny tiny."

He laughed. "What can I say, you're educating me in the subtle art of anticipation. But just so I know when you say thin, do you mean…*fine*, or is thin code for see-through?"

It was Eleanor's turn to laugh. It was going to be fun living with this man. "Well, I've had mine a *long* time, and it's been washed a lot, so…"

"And will I be getting a chance to see this transparent shift?"

Eleanor's pulse suddenly drummed in her head and pounded behind her rib cage. This was the moment. "Yes. My answer is yes."

There was a long silence and she pictured him staring at the ceiling, all shaggy and whiskered, a smile on his face.

"Really?"

"Really."

"In the spare room or…?"

His words from the other night came back to her. *I am at your service.* She swallowed. "No. Not the spare room."

"Oh thank God for that."

The relief in his voice was audible. "But it's just a trial, Bodie. *For a month.* If all goes well *then* we'll talk about applying for a marriage licence and visiting the registry office."

The whole idea was an affront to her romantic sensibilities, but given the circumstances…

"Yes, okay, fine. A trial for a month," he agreed readily and Eleanor breathed a sigh of relief. "Can you get a late checkout tomorrow?"

"Yes."

"Good. I'll pick you up after training. See you at one."

Eleanor's stomach was as jittery as a kid's on Christmas morning just thinking about it.

"Wear those pantaloons."

Her inner thighs quivered in an entirely different kind of jittery. "I'll be the girl in the foyer with the pantaloons."

"And I'll be the guy with the massive erection."

Eleanor laughed again as he rang off, almost giddy with her decision to cut loose. One o'clock tomorrow.

Which gave her plenty of time to get vagazzled!

…

She didn't wear the pantaloons. To his credit, he didn't look too crestfallen, and within fifteen minutes of leaving the hotel they were pulling into the underground car park of Bodie's apartment block in Redfern.

The inner city suburb had undergone massive

gentrification in recent years and was now quite the trendy place to live, its troubled past and indigenous heritage slowly being blended *and* whitewashed by development.

"Well, this is it." Bodie slid back the heavy iron door that opened into his apartment. "It's not a grand homestead on a cattle station, but the view's not bad."

Not bad was an understatement. Eleanor kicked off her shoes, her gaze drawn to the flood of light from the four massive floor-to-ceiling arched windows opposite the city skyline, the proud stalk of the iconic Centrepoint Tower glowing gold in the sunshine.

"It used to be an old warehouse," he said as he dragged her two large suitcases behind him. "I bought it a few years back. It's a little far from Henley, but I fell in love with the building and how they'd kept all the old fixtures. It's worth the morning traffic hassles."

"It's…"

Eleanor turned around in the middle of the huge open room, taking in the very masculine space. The exposed brick of the walls, the pipes and ducting criss-crossing the open space above their heads, the polished concrete floor stained with splashes of ochre and what looked like sump oil, the rich burgundy rugs.

Furniture was sparse, but what there was carried a distinctly masculine vibe. Heavy wood, dark leather, and smoky glass. The staircase that led up to a mezzanine floor in the far back right corner was gunmetal grey with metallic treads and steel wire balustrades.

Thank goodness for those windows letting in the light or the apartment would look more like something from *Game of Thrones*.

"Big."

He cocked an eyebrow. "I think the word you're after is blokey."

"It's…a little more Bronte than Austen, I'll give you that."

"Well you can bedazzle—" He wriggled his eyebrows at her and Eleanor tried to stop the heat swamping her cheeks at the disco ball surprise she had for him.

Might as well have tried to stop the tide.

"—the place as much as you want," he continued. "I was thinking at some stage, before the baby's born, we could find a place together? An apartment's no place to raise a family. Somewhere with a yard for the baby *and* for the country girl."

Eleanor quelled the riot going on inside her at Bodie's long-term plans. He was obviously prepared to commit to the long haul while she was still pinching herself that it was actually happening. There was still part of her that expected to wake up tomorrow and discover it had all been a dream.

A sexy, incredible, thrilling dream.

"Bodie…"

"I know, I know." He held up his hands in surrender but grinned, despite the warning in her voice. "I'm getting ahead of myself."

He was. If only her heart didn't do a funny little giddy up when he did.

She walked toward the windows to stop herself from turning to him and getting ahead of herself, too. "Right in front of these windows will be the perfect spot for my work area." She stepped over the line of light on the floor, her bare foot pale in the sudden spotlight. She could feel the warmth of the sun despite the filter of the glass.

"The natural light will be awesome for photos of the finished product, too. And so much space to hang the clothes."

She could see herself living here, sewing away until the light faded. Would she miss the wide open spaces of the outback? The sound of lowing cattle, the smell of hay, the scent of rain hitting dirt? The far horizons, the night sky?

The hustle and bustle of daily life on a cattle property?

Maybe.

Had she ever thought she'd live in the city? *No.* But unlike a lot of country people, she'd always *loved* the city. Maybe it was all the historical romances she'd read set in the *ton* in London, but travelling to Sydney had always felt like an adventure into the kind of culture that fascinated her.

And there weren't too many historical exhibitions that travelled out to Bungindally! Not to mention, she had to shop for her fabric online back home, but now she could actually visit the retailers whenever she wanted and buy off the shelf. She could haunt antique shops for lace and other fabrics.

"Speaking of sewing," Bodie interrupted her thoughts. "I'll just go grab your boxes from the car."

She looked over her shoulder at him. He was still standing in the spot she'd left him, his hands in the front pockets of his knee-length basketball shorts. His expression searched hers for what she thought might be signs of her approval.

He wanted her to like his place, to want to be here with him. Her heart fluttered.

"They'll wait." She held out her hand. "Come and show me your place first."

Chapter Nine

Bodie was nervous as he showed her around the converted warehouse he called home. Not that there was a whole lot to show. It was mostly just a big empty area with two spare bedrooms at the far end of the space separated by a bathroom. The decorator he'd hired to outfit the place had used furniture to block off zones.

Couches, a coffee table and a long, sleek unit for the television denoted the living area. A heavy mahogany table with matching high back chairs, the dining area. The long black marble kitchen bench, stools on one side, delineated the kitchen.

He wanted Eleanor to like where she was living, but seeing it through her eyes he wasn't so sure she would. His teammates loved it, but Eleanor was a woman. A woman into flouncy dresses, pretty colours, tactile fabrics—satin, ribbons, lace—frilly Victorian lingerie. She liked *froth* and this place was whatever the hell was the opposite of that.

It was the anti-froth.

Hell, it looked like it could have been an eighteenth-century sweat shop in a past life. His plans to find a home for them fermented in his brain a little more.

"You want a drink?" he asked as she ran her hands hypnotically over the sleek marble top of the kitchen bench.

"What have you got?"

Bodie opened the sleek black door of the fridge. Crap. Beer and more beer. No wine. Not that she could drink that. No soft drink either. In fact, there wasn't even much food.

"Umm…" He glanced at her over his shoulder and grimaced. "Water?"

She was wearing jeans and a deep green corset style shirt that sat like a T-shirt on her back and arms and hips, but the front panel was green satin with black ribbon lacing that had been pulled taut and tempting across her breasts.

It was distracting as fuck.

He'd wanted to unlace the damn thing from the second he'd laid eyes on her. She may not have stuck to the pantaloons promise but he'd stuck to his. His erection had been so swift and powerful he'd almost blacked out in that bloody foyer.

She smiled and shook her head, her wild, tangly hair barely contained in the big plastic claw at the back of her head.

"Water's fine. Looks like I might need to do some grocery shopping tomorrow, though."

Bodie pulled a beer out of the fridge. "Yeah, sorry about that, I usually just get some kind of delivery." He twisted the top off his beer and set it on the counter before grabbing a glass out of a high cupboard and placing it under the chilled water dispenser on the door of the fridge.

"I thought you guys were supposed to eat healthy."

He handed her the glass then a clipboard with what appeared to be an extensive menu on it. "It's proper gourmet stuff. Delivered to my door." He put his hand on his heart. "Only the best."

She scanned the menu. “Hmm. Maybe I *won’t* go shopping tomorrow.”

Bodie shrugged. “Fine by me.” He took a swig of his beer. It was cool and bitter, just the way he liked it. Nothing like a cold beer after a gruelling workout. And it gave him something to do with his hands other than pulling the tie on the lacing that crisscrossed her cleavage.

“That’s one of the best things about a city.” She sighed as she placed the clipboard down and took a sip of her water. “No gourmet restaurants out our way. And even if there were, they wouldn’t deliver out to the property. It’d be cold by the time it got there anyway.”

He studied her over the rim of his beer bottle. Was he imagining that wistful lilt to her tone? Was she missing home already? “What did your parents say?”

Her gaze flicked to his for a moment and held for a beat or two before glancing away, her face bathed in light from the windows as she stared out.

“Eleanor?”

She glanced at him. “I didn’t tell them.”

Bodie frowned, placing the bottle on the bench top with a light *tink*. “Where do they think you are now?”

“With my friend Miriam who lives in Wollongong.”

A skitter of unease crawled through Bodie’s veins. “Okay.”

“I *will* tell them. I just…”

Bodie nodded. “You’re just hedging your bets?”

She was seeing how it worked out for a couple of weeks before she said anything. He couldn’t blame her for it, but it bugged him nonetheless.

“No.”

“Okay, then what? You think they’ll be mad?” he asked. “That they’ll come down here and drag you home?”

She laughed. “Hardly. They’re my parents, not my jailers.

I'm twenty-six. I can come and go as I please. Stay with whomever I want."

"And have you ever abruptly changed your plans before?"

"Well…no."

"And how'd they take that?"

"They were…surprised. But I wasn't asking their permission, Bodie. I was just informing them I wasn't going to be home as planned."

"Because you were staying with your friend. Miriam."

"Well…I actually told them that I was going to stay on with a friend, and they *assumed* it was Miriam and I…"

"Didn't disabuse them of the notion."

"No."

"Eleanor." Bodie shook his head. "I can't go to training every morning and see Ryder and not tell him you're staying with me. He's going to be pissed enough at me for sleeping with you, he's probably going to *kill* me for getting you pregnant. I can't compound all that by acting like you're not in bed with me every night. I don't want to lie to him like that."

"I'm sorry. I know it puts you in an awkward position."

She slid her hand along the bench top toward him. It didn't reach, so Bodie met her halfway, their fingers twining.

"I will tell them." She beseeched him with her eyes, and there was something in them that Bodie knew was going to suck him right into whatever she was selling. "I just… Can I have a few days to wrap my head around it first?"

It didn't seem an unreasonable request. It wouldn't have been, had Bodie not known Ryder. But he did. And this had the potential for biting him on the ass. "Eleanor…"

"I'll tell them on the weekend." She moved her hand from his and slid off her stool, walking around to his side of the bench and sidling up to him, her body almost touching his. "Please?"

She leaned into him, rising on her tiptoes, sliding her arms around his neck, and Bodie's senses filled with the familiar orange blossom scent of her as he filled his palms with her ass.

"Are you trying to seduce me, Miss Davis?"

She buzzed her mouth against his and whispered, "I don't know, I haven't done it before. How am I doing?"

Bodie groaned in appreciation at the torturous brush of her lips and the saucy tease of her words. "Not bad." The fact that he was providing so many of her firsts was full-on caveman, beating-his-chest, dragging-his-knuckles satisfying.

He opened his mouth, capturing hers, eradicating the torturous playful brush, spinning it into a deep, slow exploration that had his heart pounding and his dick hard in seconds. The low hum of her approval buzzed to his groin in one hot lick.

She pulled out of the kiss, and he liked that he could put that expression on her face. Her gaze not quite focused. Her mouth wet and crushed. "Why haven't you shown me your bedroom yet?"

"I was trying to be a gentleman."

She smiled in a sexily unfocused way, and it grabbed him by the balls. "I thought we'd already established you weren't a gentleman."

Bodie remembered his starring performance in *Bodie Jerks Off for Eleanor.* "Oh yeah, that's right." He grinned as his cock got harder. "Well, maybe I was just trying to be on my best behaviour for your first day? Show you my impeccable manners."

"And what if I told you I had a little surprise for you that's going to make you forget your own name, let alone the quaint notion of manners?"

Bodie had no idea what that might be. But his dick turned to granite at the possibilities, and he sure as fuck wanted to find out. He kissed her hard and fast, grabbed her hand, and yanked. “Let’s go.”

She laughed as he half ushered, half dragged her along behind him, pushing her in front of him as they hit the stairs, his pulse leaping as she took them two at a time. He stayed right on her ass.

“So this is the bedroom.” He gestured with his hand, surprisingly out of breath for a man who regularly ran over ten kilometres a day. Not that his state of breathlessness had anything to do with the short bolt across his apartment.

“I chose this corner because the fixtures—”

“Fixtures blah, blah, blah,” she muttered, cutting him off as she spun in his arms and plastered herself against him, her mouth seeking his, moaning as they met.

Bodie groaned, his hands ploughing into the thick tangle of her hair to steady them as he bent to her, kissing her hard, his hands finding her ass again, his heart beating like a drum in his chest.

“I missed you,” he murmured, breaking off to slide kisses to her ear then down her neck as he toed off his shoes.

It had been an exercise in self control not to call on her every night these past few days. To knock on her hotel door and ask her to let him in. Beg if he had to. Promise her whatever she wanted for a night in her arms.

Lying in his bed these past couple of months thinking she was twelve-hundred kilometres away had put a mental lock on his cravings. Knowing she was a fifteen-minute drive from him? That had been agony.

Her hands tunnelled under his shirt, dragging it up, and he helped her pull it over his head. “God…” She laid her hands flat on his pecs before smoothing them down to his abs, causing a rapid chain reaction in the muscles below the flesh. “If I was a poet, I’d write an ode to your chest.”

Bodie chuckled, his attention firmly fixed on her chest.

"How *does* this thing come undone?"

"Bow. At the bottom."

Wild horses couldn't have stopped Bodie from yanking it. The lacing, already under strain from the pressure of her breasts, loosened and widened in the blink of an eye, the tightness unravelling like the pop of a champagne cork, and in a flash she'd whipped it up and off.

She wasn't wearing a bra. Her gorgeous full breasts swung soft and free. The pale pink nipples hardened before his eyes.

"*Holy. Fuck*. I'm *never* going to get tired of that sight."

He ducked his head, his mouth already coated in saliva as it landed on the right nipple. She cried out and he dragged his tongue over it back and forth, back and forth, revelling in how she arched into him and dug her nails into his back.

His little hell-cat.

Bodie released his mouthful to the air, leaning back to admire his handiwork, the engorged nipple blushed more brown than pink now. Red marks where his whiskers had scraped the flesh of her breast should have horrified him, but it filled his beating heart with a primal roar of possession.

"I like marking you."

Her nostrils flared at his admission, her whiskey eyes glowing almost feral. Oh yeah. *She liked it, too.*

She launched herself at him, her breasts squashed against him, the hard points of her nipples pressing into the wall of his chest as she yanked on his neck and kissed him. Bodie took what she gave him and demanded more, thrusting his tongue inside her mouth, chasing every whimper, driving deeper, wanting more.

Suddenly, her hands were pushing into the waist band of his shorts, taking his underwear with them, pushing them down off his hips and thighs and he was helping, wriggling his legs as he kissed her and somehow between the two of them they were off and he was naked and she was pushing him backward toward his bed. The mattress was suddenly behind his knees and then his ass was on the bed and she was standing between his legs topless, her skin so pale, looking down at him, her eyes superglued to his cock like it was a particularly exotic ingredient and she was deciding how to cook it.

It twitched at her intense scrutiny, his balls tightened. His gaze dropped to her jeans, wondering how come he was naked and she wasn't.

What the fuck had he been doing all this time?

"Is your surprise under there?" He pointed at the zipper.

After long, satisfying seconds, she dragged her eyes off what lay between his legs. The woman was good for his ego. "It could be."

He tutted. "Did you get a Brazilian, Miss Davis?" He'd laughed when she'd gone on about not being vagazzled enough for a *guy like him* but obviously she'd been worried about it.

Her Mona Lisa smile clashed with the wild flush of her cheeks. He loved how easily she embarrassed. "I might have."

"Well come on, woman." He raised himself up on his elbows. "Do I get to see it or not?" Her blush deepened and she dropped her gaze. He lowered his voice an octave. "Take them off, Eleanor."

She lifted her eyes to meet his, took a calming breath, and reached for her zip, pulling the tab slowly down. He felt every tooth of the zip slip free from its hold like an electric shock to his balls. By the time she was wriggling her hips and pushing her jeans off her legs they ached like crazy.

She straightened, her breasts swaying with the movement, her hands crossed in front of herself like she'd done in Bungindally. "Let me see."

Slowly, she dropped her hands.

Bodie's breath escaped in a rush as his gaze zeroed in on

the apex of her thighs. He hadn't expected to see complete smoothness. Maybe some kind of landing strip left behind. He'd been with a woman once who'd had her pubic hair trimmed into the shape of a heart and dyed hot pink.

But he *did not* expect to see what was there. He didn't expect sparkle. A provocative message just for him.

In silver and blue diamantes—or whatever the hell it was they used in nether regions for a little bit of pizzazz—the words, *Ruck Me*, stood out in thick capitals like a flashing neon sign against the smooth baldness of her mons.

If he hadn't already been hard enough to crack nuts he would be now. Slowly, he levered himself into an upright position, his hands sliding onto his thighs.

So *that* was vagazzling.

"You like?"

He lifted his gaze, her face a fiery red now, her expression one of tortured insecurity. "Like?" That was far too bland a description for the riot going on inside his testicles right now. "Honey, I think I just came."

She smiled, the line of her shoulders relaxing, her breasts swaying with the motion. "It's…shiny," she said, almost apologetically, her voice unsteady.

And not from embarrassment. From arousal. She was as turned on as him.

Bodie laughed. "Like a disco ball." He lowered his eyes to the words again, staring at her, marvelling at her. "Not very Victorian."

She gave a soft snort. "Only because they didn't think of it first. They were a pretty depraved bunch."

"I know." He dragged his gaze up her body. "I've seen some of their pornography."

"Really?" She quirked an eyebrow.

He waved a dismissive hand. "Long story." He crooked his finger. "Come here. I want a closer look."

She took the two steps required to put her back between his knees which brought him eye level with her sparkly new surprise. His nostrils flared as they filled with the citrusy scent of her skin and the wild musky aroma of aroused woman.

"So…is that meant as an instruction?"

She shook her head. "It's an order."

Bodie grinned, sliding his hands onto her hips and jerking them closer. "Yes ma'am." And he leaned forward.

"Oh no no no." She pushed hard against his shoulders, and Bodie growled in frustration as he looked at her.

"It's my turn to do that."

She planted a hand in the centre of his chest and gave him a shove. He collapsed back onto the mattress, his cock straining against the flat surface of his belly as she looked at it once again like she was preparing to devour it.

She planted a knee on the mattress between his legs. "Shuffle back."

Bodie shuffled back, his eyes glued to the sway of her breasts and the *sexy as fuck* wink of shiny jewels between her legs as she followed him up the bed on all fours. He stopped when his head hit the pillow. So did she, settling on her haunches between his legs.

"Do you mind if I just…" His quads jumped as her hands smoothed over them. Her gaze locked onto his dick. His balls tightened and pulled a little higher. "Play a little."

Bodie shook his head. If she wanted to get up and personal with his anatomy, he wasn't going to object. "Be my guest."

Her finger, cool as ice and twice as smooth, landed on the hypersensitive tissue where the thick bulb of his head met his shaft. She ran it from the tip all the way down to the root and Bodie bit back a groan.

"I want to give you a…" She stopped and the muscles in Bodie's ass contracted. "Perform oral sex on you."

Oh Christ. His dick bucked and she hadn't even touched it this time. Her primness was way more of a turn on than it should be. "You can say blow job. I won't tell anyone."

She blushed but said it anyway. "Blow job." She blushed some more. "But I don't want to screw it up."

Bodie laughed, which cut out abruptly as two fingers stroked down his length. "I don't think there's *any* way you could screw up a blow job, unless you bite it."

She laughed. "No biting. Check. But…do I swallow or not? What do you think?"

Bodie's eyes almost rolled back in his head as her fingers curled around his cock and slid up and down, taking their damn time exploring the length of him. He fisted his hands into the sheets. "I think you should never ask a guy that question. They're always going to want you to swallow."

"My sister Lisa says sperm tastes disgusting. That she almost considered switching teams the first and only time she tried it."

"Well…yeah." He shut his eyes and panted against the urge to thrust into her hand as her thumb rubbed maddeningly across the head. His heart banged hard against his ribs, his skin was hot enough to fall from his bones. "I gotta admit, I wouldn't like to swallow it."

"But I feel like I should at least *try* it. Make up my own mind. I mean you…did it to me. Which was…well…let's just say I am *very* grateful that you did, but…" She shook her head. "I really wouldn't do that if I was a guy."

Bodie managed to prise his eyes open as her hand slid up and down. "I loved it. I've dreamed about going down on you just about every night since." Her pace faltered and her gorgeous lips parted and he wanted them on him *so fucking bad*.

"You were very good at it…I think."

He sucked in a ragged breath, the sway of her breasts

more mesmerizing than a Victorian hypnotist's watch. "I've never had any complaints." The fact that he'd been the only man to ever put his mouth to her pounded like an anthem through his veins.

"That's what I mean. I don't bring the same level of expertise to this that you did. My technique—"

"Eleanor."

Bodie wouldn't have normally interrupted any woman with her hand on his cock, but his body was pulled taut from the strain of keeping himself in check. He'd never worried about premature ejaculation before but between the swing of her gorgeous tits, the vagazzling, and the somehow incredibly sexy clinical discussion about blow jobs, his balls were so primed she could probably just whistle for him to come and he would.

"You should just suck it already." His voice sounded as if it had rumbled up from the centre of the earth. "I don't care about your technique or whether you swallow or not. You can pull off, you can spit it out. I really don't care. Just *please,* if you could put it in your mouth now... You're killing me."

She bent then, so swift and sure, her hot mouth sliding over him, and Bodie's hips jerked off the bed. "*Fuuuck*."

Her tongue swirled around and around his head and he groaned, his eyes shutting as he sunk his hands into her hair. The hot slide of her mouth, all the way down his shaft as far as she could go, and the firm suction as she withdrew, popped stars behind his eyes.

Every glide on and off was perfect. She was perfect. "*Jesus*, that's good."

She hummed her satisfaction against his head as she withdrew, and the sound vibrated down his shaft and sizzled through his balls. "Should I...suck your testicles?"

Bodie angled his head off the pillow, his gaze meeting hers. He was excruciatingly aware of the wet state of her mouth as it hovered just above the wet state of cock. Her hesitant request slipping from lips that had been gorging on him a second ago was like a nuclear charge to his groin.

"Christ yes. You should *definitely* suck my testicles."

And then her hot mouth was on his balls sucking them both into the cavern of her mouth. He groaned, his head flopping back against the pillow, his hands sliding from her hair as he lost all muscle control. She rolled them in her hand and laved them with her tongue, tripping every pleasure sensor he possessed.

His heart hammered way beyond his healthy cardio range as she played between his legs until he didn't think he could take it anymore. Just when he thought his heart might burst through his chest, she stopped. His balls slid from the wet heat of her mouth as her tongue and lips slid hot and urgent down his shaft again, her nails pressing into the flesh covering the hard bones of his hips.

They bucked in her hold. He couldn't help it, couldn't stop them as her mouth enveloped him. But it only seemed to embolden her and the noises she made at the back of her throat as she took him deeper *and deeper* sunk hot talons into his balls.

"Eleanor…*Jesus*." He was going to come. He had to warn her. "Eleanor…" He lost his train of thought, gripping hold of his sanity to try again. "I'm about two seconds from coming." His chest heaved and his breath felt like wet sand in his lungs. "If you want off, it better be now."

But she didn't pull off, she didn't stop, she just dug her fingers harder into his hips and moaned. The noise shot down his shaft and vibrated through his balls and pushed him over the edge.

He came—*loud*—his hands fisting in the sheets as his hips thrust again, pumping deep in the back of her throat and holding there as he spilled his load. The triumph of her moan, the cut of her fingernails, were all lost in the hot greedy suck of her mouth and the undulation of her throat.

He shut his eyes as the hard edge of bliss took him to another dimension, twirled him around, then pushed him out the other side.

Chapter Ten

When Bodie came to, she was sitting on her haunches between his legs again looking pleased with herself.

She grinned. "Hey."

"Sorry." He shot her a self-deprecating smile. "I think I blacked out there for a moment."

Her laughter was almost giddy. Yeah. She was *very* pleased with herself.

And sexy as hell, looking all accomplished like she'd graduated from sex ed with full honours and she knew it. He laughed, too, his dick surprisingly firm despite the orgasm.

Atta boy.

"So…what's the verdict?" He cocked an eyebrow which was about all he was capable of at the moment anyway. "Swallowing yea or nay?"

Frankly, Bodie couldn't give a shit. As long as she still wanted to suck his dick in some capacity, he'd take whatever happy ending she was willing to give him.

She wrinkled her nose as if she was judging the bouquet of a fine wine instead of the taste of his spunk. As if she wasn't sitting there stark naked with *Ruck Me* twinkling at him from between her legs. "Well I wouldn't order it on a menu, but I didn't hate it. Honestly, I think you were so far back when you climaxed, I didn't get much of a taste."

"Oh really?" He smiled. "So you might need to study the conundrum a little more?"

Deadpan she said, "I think I need a much bigger sample size."

Bodie laughed. "I'm sure I can oblige."

He pulled her down beside him, and he loved how natural it felt for her to snuggle her body into his. How right it felt for her hand to slide over the top of his heart. Bodie stroked her arm, and her skin roughed to goose bumps beneath his slow caress.

"I feel like I must apologise for my speed. I don't usually blow my load so quickly, but I seem to be making a habit of it with you. It's like I'm fifteen all over again."

In his defence, he didn't usually have a gorgeous, generous, curvy woman eager to try out her newfound sexual appetite on him, either.

She stirred, propping herself up on her elbow and looking down at him. "Being able to make you lose control so quickly makes me so hot I can barely see straight."

"Hot, huh?" Bodie smiled. "In that case, I'll let my inner fifteen-year-old run wild."

She smiled as she slid down and rolled on her side. "Spoon me."

Bodie snuggled in behind her, his chest to her back, his thighs cradling hers, her naked ass pushed into groin, his still very interested cock resting against the cleft of her buttocks. He slid his hand over her waist to cup the soft rise of her belly where his child—*his child*—was growing.

"How does it feel? Knowing there's a baby in there?"

She placed her hand over top of his. "Surreal and kinda

hard to believe, really, when all I have is six positive test kits, a few days of breast tenderness, and some vague, occasional nausea."

Bodie laughed. "You took *six* tests?"

"Seven if you count the one the doctor did."

He dropped a kiss on her shoulder. "I wish I'd been there."

She squeezed his hand. "You're here now."

He was. And he wasn't going anywhere, either. He was going to use these next few weeks to prove it. Open himself up. Let her get to know him, so she knew he was a man of his word. And he could get to know her, too.

Of course, he already knew a lot about her. Where she came from, the names of her parents and siblings—particularly her *brother*—and that she lived and worked on the family cattle property. He knew she was also an accomplished seamstress and businesswoman and had an encyclopaedic knowledge of all things nineteenth century. He knew she was shy and sweet and when she got nervous she talked too much.

And she was carrying his child.

"Eleanor." His lips brushed her nape as he sounded out her name. He'd told her the night they'd met that it suited her and he'd meant it. "You said it was your grandmother's name?"

She sighed and snuggled her ass in closer. "Yes. She lived with us until she died when I was fourteen. I take after her, short and round, and she introduced me to Georgette Heyer when I was ten. I was hooked." Her chest expanded against his in a deep sigh. "And she taught me how to sew. She was the only one who called me Eleanor. Until you."

"Why *does* everyone call you Nell?"

"My brother couldn't say Eleanor properly when he was little." Her response sounded rote, as if she'd told the story a thousand times already. "Ryder could only say Nell, and it just kinda stuck."

Ryder. Bodie tensed at the mention of his name, his sense of guilt from earlier revisiting.

"I don't really mind it for the most part," she continued. "But I wish it had been spelled with an i. Like Jane Austen's Elinor in *Sense and Sensibility.* I think I'm probably most like her out of all Austen's characters so it seems kinda fitting. I went on a campaign as a kid to convince my mother to change it by deed poll but…I couldn't persuade her."

"Hmmm." His lips buzzed her neck. "Well I like it, however it's spelled," he murmured in low, hushed tones. "Or do you prefer Miss Davis?" She squirmed and his lips curved. "Oh yeah, *that* makes you hot, huh?"

She gave a half laugh. "I think you can take it as your mere existence makes me hot."

Bodie chuckled and rubbed his dick, back to full throttle again, along the seam of her ass. "Right back at you, honey."

She slid her arm up behind her, ploughing it into the hair at the back of his head and holding him there. "You *are* a fifteen-year-old boy."

"What can I say? You make me so fucking horny." The hand low on her belly headed south, the bareness of her, the scrape of her jewels an erotic reminder of the lengths she'd gone for him.

His cock hardened to stone.

"Your turn," he murmured, his hand grabbing her top thigh, urging it back over his, grunting in satisfaction as her foot locked in behind his calves. His fingers slid immediately into the slickness between her legs, taking advantage of her splayed position, zeroing in on the nub already engorged.

"How long can *you* last?" he whispered in her ear and she gasped and arched her back as he squeezed the hard bead in a pincer grip.

"Not very long if you keep doing that."

"What? This?"

Bodie did it again and again before easing back to a circling motion, pressing harder and closer with each revolution. She was moaning in his arms, panting, everything so hot and slick between her legs now that his cock had slid into place, gliding back and forth along the swollen seam of her sex.

"Please…" Eleanor's hips flexed as she rode the thick edge of his cock, her body telling him exactly where she really needed it.

"Please, what, *Miss Davis?*" He whispered it deliberately, breathing it into her ear. "What do you want?"

"Please, I want…I need…"

She was grinding so hard against him the friction between their bodies would have been enough to light a New Year's Eve fireworks display. She was trembling in his arms.

Close, so close.

"You can tell me." He kept his voice to a whisper, his finger on her clit easing off a little. He wanted her to come the second he entered her, not before.

"Bodie."

God, he was probably going to go to *all* the kinds of hell for wanting to corrupt her, but he wanted to hear her say *fuck*. Hear that dirty word coming from her prim, little mouth.

"It's okay, you can say, *fuck me*."

"*Bodie*."

It came out as a growl this time and damn if that didn't make him harder. "Come on, honey, you can do it. You know you want to say it." He'd seen how her nostrils flared every time he used crude language. He teased the head of his cock at her entrance for incentive. "I know how much saying *fuck* turns you on."

She cried out then a deep, dark bellow. "Bodie!" She sunk her nails into the back of his neck. "Fuck me. Now!"

Bodie surged into her on a roar of triumph, gloriously bareback, his fingers flying over her clit, holding her tight as she broke apart in his arms, her snug, wet heat clenching around him as her orgasm burgeoned. He gritted his teeth, fighting against the pull of his own climax, his hips bucking, ramming inside her, pushing her higher and higher until he couldn't any longer, spilling inside her, joining her in the rapture.

"Christ." He breathed heavily into her neck as they came down in the aftermath, his pulse still a faint echo in his ears. "I think I'm regressing. I'm getting quicker."

She laughed, low and raspy and clearly not concerned at all about the speed of their orgasms. "Maybe I'm just getting better?"

Bodie chuckled, disturbing the tiny dark hairs at her neck with the puff of air. What a thought. Eleanor growing more and more sexually powerful. The magnificence of it was breathtaking and a hot illicit tingle shot straight up his spine.

He smiled, his lip buzzing the side of her neck. "Sounds like I created a monster."

"*Fucking* A."

Bodie laughed. *Bring it on.*

• • •

Eleanor's bliss lasted three days.

Three days of lazy lie-ins while Bodie was at training—a beautiful novelty for a country girl—then rising to catch an art exhibition or a visiting museum show or passing a few hours haunting material shops. Then some more long, lazy hours in bed with Bodie in the afternoon, into the night.

No matter how tired he was from the physical exertion of his training, he stepped through the heavy steel of the front door and he was reaching for her—if she didn't beat him to it first.

He'd even sacrificed poker night, despite her urging him not to. She didn't want to disrupt his usual routine, and she'd discovered his Netflix account—a luxury for a girl from a place where the internet was basic at best. She'd told him she could occupy herself for a few hours. But he'd just shook his head and pulled off his shirt, and all of her protests died on her lips.

But then Thursday arrived and their quiet evening in with some gourmet takeaway took a *very* bad turn. A knock at their front door alerted them to the arrival of their meal.

"That'll be the delivery guy," Bodie called from the bedroom.

She was in the kitchen. "I'll go." She hummed as she crossed the expansive space she still wasn't quite used to.

"No, I'll get it," he said from the top of the stairs, and she rolled her eyes as she unlatched the door.

Bodie didn't like her opening it because he said it was too heavy for a *woman in her condition.* If it hadn't melted her heart every time he said it, she'd have probably been cranky about it. It *was* a stupidly heavy door, but she was pregnant, not an invalid.

She braced herself as she rolled the solid hunk of metal back on its tracks. But it wasn't the delivery guy.

"Nell?"

Ryder's brows beetled beneath the rim of his standard black akubra. His puzzled expression took in the old Sydney Smoke jersey of Bodie's, which, thankfully, almost reached her knees, and her bare feet. Beside him, his fiancée Juliet blinked, owl-like.

Well…damn.

"Honey."

She shut her eyes as Bodie's voice grew closer. This was not the way she'd planned to tell her brother about her new relationship.

"How many times do I have to tell you not to open the—"

Ryder's gaze switched to Bodie as he came into sight, the creases in his forehead deepening as he obviously tried to compute what the hell was going on. Juliet appeared to have caught on pretty quickly, if the hand she slid onto Ryder's forearm was any indication.

Ryder looked from one to the other before glaring at Eleanor. "I thought you were at Miriam's?"

"Surprise." She shot him a fake smile, knowing humour was the last thing warranted here but hoping that one day they could all laugh about this.

"I think you guys better come in." Bodie stepped to the side and gestured for them to enter.

Ryder didn't move, glancing at a bare-chested Bodie in nothing but his jeans with the top button undone. Eleanor hoped he wouldn't guess Bodie was going commando. Or that she was, for that matter.

"What the fuck is going on?" he demanded.

Juliet sighed. "Not here, cowboy." And she half dragged Ryder into the apartment. "Sorry," she apologised on her way in, kissing both Bodie and Eleanor on the cheek. "We just thought we'd pop in for a drink on our way into the city. We should have…called first."

Eleanor shot Bodie a furtive look. The expression on his face was closed. She knew this was exactly the kind of thing he'd been dreading, but he dredged up a smile for her as they both turned to face her brother.

"Why are you here, Nell?"

Bodie slid his arm around her waist and pulled her close. "She lives here now. We're together."

Her heart skipped a beat at Bodie staking his claim. She should be trying to explain about the month trial, trying to qualify Bodie's assertion, but everything, including her will, had gone a little weak.

Bodie was *so* getting laid as soon as her brother left.

"What?" Ryder's jaw looked like it was about to shatter as he stared at Bodie's show of possession. "No." He shook his head. "That's crazy. She's a virgin, for God's sake."

Eleanor rolled her eyes. As much as she'd often fantasised about living in the nineteenth century, she could never have coped with this male patriarchal crap. Bodie opened his mouth to say something but Eleanor wasn't going to let her brother lord it over her.

"I hate to break it to you, but I'm not anymore."

If it had been happening to anyone else, the look on Ryder's face might have been comical. "Oh my God." He glared at Bodie. "You popped her cherry?"

Juliet winced, so did Eleanor, but she was not going to stand by and let Bodie and her brother have this conversation as if she wasn't in the room at all.

"Yes. At your engagement party." She wasn't ashamed of what had happened.

Ryder gave another comical male double-take. "You *slept* with my sister at my *engagement party*?"

"I didn't know she was your sister."

Ryder cut his annoyed glare to Eleanor. "You didn't *tell* him you were my sister?"

"No."

"Why the fuck not?"

"Because I didn't think he'd sleep with me if he knew."

Eleanor announced it calmly, noting how Juliet pressed her lips together like she was trying to suppress a smile. Ryder, on the other hand, looked like he wanted a bucket of brain bleach.

"I absolutely would not have slept with her if I'd known."

"Oh my God." A sudden clearly horrifying thought occurred to Ryder. "*She* made those nail marks? No—" He held up his hand. "Don't answer that, I don't want to know."

Bodie wisely kept his mouth shut as Ryder looked like he wanted to *drink* the brain bleach now. Not that he needed to say anything with Eleanor's blush pretty much confirming it. Ryder dragged his hat off his head and started to pace as if the information would be more palatable while he was walking.

"So…you guys have been…screwing around for a couple of months now?"

"No." Eleanor watched her brother pace. "It was just that night, and then I looked him up when I landed in town last week."

"And you—" Ryder stopped mid-pace and glared at Bodie. "Couldn't keep your grubby hands to yourself."

Bodie tensed beside her and a swift bubble of rage exploded in Eleanor's chest. "Don't talk to him like that."

Ryder glowered but started pacing again. "So, what now? You've known him for less than a fucking week and you're shacking up with him?"

"Yes," she snapped. Eleanor was far too angry now to clarify the situation. Let her brother stew on that.

Ryder gave a harsh laugh, pulling up again. "Do you have any idea how many women this guy has slept with?"

"Dude." Bodie's voice was laced with warning as he stood practically rigid beside her now.

Rage was like ice in Eleanor's veins now. She loved Ryder, but his hypocrisy was stunning and she wouldn't put up with his holier-than-thou attitude. "Considering he was in a long-term relationship for *five years*, probably nowhere near as many as you."

Juliet laughed. "She's got you there, cowboy."

Ryder shot his fiancée an exasperated look that clearly said *you're supposed to be on my side.* Juliet just shrugged and smiled some more. "I don't want you to be just another woman on his rebound list."

Eleanor felt the tension jump in every muscle of Bodie's body, primed to spring into action. "It's *not* like that," he said, through clenched teeth.

She squeezed his waist to stop him from lunging at Ryder, even though it was exactly what her brother deserved.

Ryder snorted. "Sure."

Eleanor's patience snapped loud enough to be heard on the other side of the planet. She'd had just about as much as she could take of her brother's carry on. "I'm sorry, but did I miss something?" she demanded. "He *is* your best friend, isn't he?"

"He *was*."

"Have I not heard you say a thousand times what a great bloke he is?"

Ryder crossed his arms and stared at her with a sullen set to his jaw, not happy with her application of logic. "Bodie's the best," Juliet confirmed when Ryder clearly wasn't going to answer.

Ryder shot her another exasperated look but she just smiled at him pleasantly as Bodie nodded and said, "Damn straight I am."

"So if he's a great bloke, if he's *the best,* and he's good enough to be *your* best friend, why is it so shocking that I'd like him, that I'd want to be with him? Or is it too hard to wrap your head around anyone wanting your ugly duckling sister?"

Bodie squeezed her waist as Ryder shoved a hand through his hair. "Jesus…Nell…of course not."

"*Fuck,* Ryder." Her brother's eyebrows shot up at her profanity. She'd shocked herself, too, but she wasn't sorry. "My name is *Eleanor.*"

Ryder shook his head like he couldn't take in any of what was going down. He started to pace again. "I just don't understand it. This is so…crazy and sudden and just not *you…*" His gaze searched hers. "I mean, what's the fucking rush? Unless you're—"

He stopped pacing abruptly, and Eleanor saw the exact moment the penny dropped. "*Jeezus…*you're pregnant, aren't you?"

Maybe Bodie, the poker player, could have bluffed it out, but Eleanor was lousy at cards. She dropped her gaze, but it was too late. She could tell he'd seen the truth.

Ryder cut his gaze to Bodie, the glare back. "She's *pregnant*?"

Bodie shifted uncomfortably. "Yes."

Ryder took a step toward Bodie and adrenaline shot through Eleanor's system. Ryder wouldn't hit his best friend and teammate, surely? Juliet slid her hand onto Ryder's arm again and he didn't advance any closer, but he clenched his hands.

"You didn't even use *condoms*?"

"Of course we did," Bodie snapped. He was clearly as done with Ryder's crap as she was.

"Christ." Ryder took a deep breath, and Eleanor felt a little sorry for him. It was rare to see Ryder at a loss. He shook his head at Bodie. "When were you going to tell me you were sleeping with my sister, man?"

Eleanor ignored the note of injury in her brother's voice. She couldn't bear the thought that she might cause a rift between Ryder and Bodie. "He wanted to tell you on Monday. I asked him to hold off until this weekend when I ring Mum and Dad to tell them of my real whereabouts."

"And when are you planning on telling them about the baby?"

"Not yet. In a few weeks. After the first trimester. So please, just don't say anything, okay?"

She appealed to him with her eyes, but Ryder didn't seem to be comprehending very much. "He won't," Juliet assured.

"They're going to worry."

Guilt twinged in her abdomen. She didn't need her brother to tell her how her parents would react. They'd be supportive of course but they *would* worry, for all the reasons Ryder was—because it was so rushed and so out of character.

But this was her life.

She raised her chin. "Just as well, I can take care of myself."

Bodie looked directly at Ryder. "They don't need to worry."

Ryder's jaw was still set tight but he seemed more resigned now as he glanced at his sister, the puff gone from his chest. "And this is what you want? What happened to romance and courtship?"

An unexpected pang of longing hit Eleanor in the chest. She'd resigned herself to the mismatch of the fantasy and her reality the day she'd decided to move in with Bodie.

Or so she'd thought.

"This is what I want." She wanted Bodie. She wanted their baby.

Ryder sighed heavily, clearly not happy. But her brother didn't get a say in her life. Neither did her parents. Ryder flicked a look at Bodie. "You shouldn't have slept with her behind my back, man."

The hard line of Bodie's shoulders relaxed as the tension in the room dialled down. "I know."

Ryder glanced at Juliet, who smiled at him sympathetically and gave his arm a squeeze. "Now that's off everyone's chests, I think we should probably leave these guys to their evening, yeah?" She smiled at Eleanor. "Sorry for interrupting your night and congratulations on your pregnancy." Juliet came forward and hugged and kissed Eleanor while both Ryder and Bodie stood stiffly. "We should get together for a coffee or something soon?"

"Oh…yes." Eleanor smiled at Juliet, surprised and pleased at the invitation. "I'd like that."

And then Juliet was dragging Ryder out of the apartment, crossing over with the food delivery guy who handed over their meal. Bodie shut the door after him, placing the food on the floor as he turned to face Eleanor, leaning against the solid metal for support.

"Well. That went well." His shoulders were slumped as he rubbed at his neck and a fresh surge of guilt washed through her system.

"I'm sorry. I know you wanted to avoid something like that."

"I'm fine." He shrugged it off like a rift with his best friend was no biggie. "Are you okay?"

She waved a dismissive hand as she moved closer to him. "Ryder will get over it. He was just blowing off steam."

"Yeah, I know." And Eleanor supposed he did know. Bodie and her brother were pretty tight, after all.

Or had been, anyway.

"But…was he right about your parents? Will they worry?"

Eleanor slid a hand onto his bare chest as soon as she was close enough. It was warm and smooth, and she couldn't believe she was the lucky woman who got to touch him like this whenever she wanted.

"They're parents. That's what they do."

His inky blue eyes darkened to indigo. "I *am* going to take care of you."

She smiled. "I know." And she raised up on her tiptoes and kissed him. She didn't need him to take care of her. As she'd told Ryder, she could take care of herself. But damn if it didn't go straight to the cockles of her romantic heart that he wanted to.

She broke off, and he groaned as he nuzzled her neck. "I feel terrible that Ryder found out like that."

Eleanor did, too. She wished it had been different, but she couldn't wind back time. She *could* help make things a little easier to bear though. Quickly, she grasped the hem of her jersey and whipped it off over the top of her head.

"Does this help?"

His eyes almost popped out of his head as he checked out every naked inch of her skin, his gaze lingering on the flashy ruck me invitation. "You know, it really does."

And then he swept her off her feet and carried her up the stairs to the loft.

Chapter Eleven

Eleanor held out for a week against Bodie's entreaty to come and watch him play. She wanted to, but things were still apparently strained between Ryder and Bodie and she wasn't sure her presence in the corporate box would smooth things over any. Add to that her social ineptness, and it had potential disaster written all over it.

It was a relief on one hand to have their relationship out in the open as far as her family went. Her parents had been puzzled and *concerned* by her out-of-character announcement, as she'd known they would be. Her father had been stilted and her mother had that disappointed tone in her voice she'd always used to good effect.

The tone that said *this is your life but I don't think you're making the best decision*.

It still made her squirm. God alone knew how much more earnest it would become when they found out she was pregnant. But they hadn't tried to talk her out of it, for which she was grateful.

Her sisters had been *agog*. They'd each rung and

exclaimed over her secrecy and congratulated her on her new boyfriend. Lisa has gone further, brandishing Bodie as a seriously hot choice to finally *do the deed* with and she hoped that Eleanor was *hitting that* like crazy.

She should have been miffed over her sister's degree of surprise, but Lisa was right, Bodie *was* seriously hot and she totally was *hitting that* like crazy.

But, as far as she was aware, no one on the team knew apart from Ryder. Bodie hadn't been keen to announce it with her brother still acting like a caveman, which meant that, unless Juliet had told the other WAGs, her presence in the corporate box would probably raise eyebrows.

Her plan was to go in the guise of Ryder's sister. She'd met a lot of the WAGs at the engagement party—although she'd felt invisible in their glamorous presence—so she was sure she could pull it off. But her nervousness in social situations wasn't as easy to bluff her way through.

In fact, by the time Eve—Griffin King's PA—was ushering her into the corporate box on game night, her mouth was so dry her tongue was practically stuck to the roof of her mouth. What was she doing? She was a shy, newly deflowered, pregnant, country-hick-book-nerd who was fluent in nineteenth century but terrible at the art of modern chit chat.

She wished Bodie was here. Bodie somehow made her forget about all those things. How could she pull this off in front of a dozen glamazons?

She thanked God she was wearing one of her many handmade corsets that gave a little nod to the steam punk style and an A-line skirt, which allowed her to wear a pair of those crotchless pantaloons that drove Bodie crazy. She stuck out like a pimple on a pumpkin amongst all the designer denim and Smoke jerseys, but Eleanor transformed into a different person in these clothes and she needed that kind of confidence.

Eve was just about to introduce Eleanor when one of the women said, "Hey, you're Ryder's sister, right? Nell?"

"Eleanor," she corrected, her pulse spiking at the sudden interest from a room full of women who looked like they'd all stepped off a Parisian catwalk.

"Eleanor." Juliet crossed the room and kissed her cheek, ushering her into the room. "I didn't know you were coming tonight. It's so good to see you again."

"Thanks," Eve said, shooting Juliet a relieved smile. "If you would do the honours? I've got to take Liam his puffer."

Eleanor watched Eve go and wished she could go with her. The older woman was all brisk efficiency instead of blinding glamour and Eleanor wanted to cling to her. "Who's Liam?" And why did they let a guy who needed an asthma puffer play rugby?

"It's Eve's sixteen-year-old son," said the woman who had first spoken. "He's the water boy at home games." She held out a glass of champagne, which Eleanor politely refused. "I'm Kathy Trimble, John's wife."

There was a dizzying round of introductions performed by Juliet. Eleanor remembered most of the faces from the engagement party and her face ached from her fixed smile. A waiter entered the box then with a platter of nibbles. Eleanor's stomach grumbled and her mouth watered. She'd felt mildly nauseated this morning and had, consequently, barely eaten.

But when the platter came her way a waft of curry hit her and nausea—sudden, hot, and bilious—left her in a cold sweat. She actually reared back from the platter, placing her hand over her mouth and nose as she clutched at her stomach with the other.

"No thank you," she managed to just choke out at the startled look on the waiter's face.

She didn't miss the speculative glances from the women,

either, and forced herself to drop both hands and smile. She could see them thinking no champagne *and* turning green at food. She could see them putting two and two together.

And getting four.

But then Juliet rescued her, dragging her over to the big floor-to-ceiling glass window, for which she was grateful, even if her legs did suddenly feel about as supportive as tin foil.

"You okay?" she asked under her breath.

Eleanor nodded. And she was. *Now.* As quickly as it had arrived, the nausea was gone and her heart rate was settling. But she sure as hell was steering clear of curry for the next thirty weeks.

She looked absently out over the lit field, a light drizzle forming a fine mist over the middle. It hadn't deterred any of the fans, though. Not if the rapidly filling stadium was any indication.

"Ball's going to be slippery," someone said.

"So will the pitch," someone else said, and there were general murmurs about injury and poor visibility.

"I love your top."

And just like that, the conversation shifted as Valerie, Griff King's daughter, a willowy redhead with freckles, complimented her. "Where did you get it from?"

Instantly, Eleanor relaxed, morphing into her kooky nineteenth-century persona, coming alive under the interest of the other women who were genuinely fascinated by her business. They asked a string of questions and Eleanor gave out half a dozen cards, which took them right up to kickoff.

"I suppose you know all there is to know about rugby, growing up with Ryder." Matilda, Tanner Stone's wife, smiled at her as they stood side by side in front of the glass. "But just holler if you want to know anything."

"Thank you. I will."

"Here they come." Harper, Dexter's wife, nodded at the

line of men running onto the field. Their baby was asleep in a pram in the back corner of the room.

"I love this bit." Lincoln Quinn's fiancée Em was close enough to the window for her bouncy caramel curls to brush the glass. "Before they all get crunched and smashed. I still can't get used to the brutality of it."

"Go hard or go home," Val quipped.

"There's Ryder," Harper said, nudging Eleanor's arm and pointing.

Eleanor could see Juliet smiling behind the rim of her champagne glass. She was the only woman in the room who knew who Eleanor was really here to see.

The women made general conversation around her as they waited for the start of the game. Eleanor tuned into the low commentary running from the wall-mounted television behind them and tried not to openly ogle Bodie who looked even hotter than usual all pumped up on the field.

The television commentators were talking about the weather and she absently wondered how heavy the rain needed to get before a game was called off. Too much longer and those uniforms were going to be clinging even more than they did now. It probably wasn't appropriate to be hoping for that.

But she made a mental note to push Bodie into the shower in his uniform.

The ring of boot against leather could be heard even from inside the box and the game commenced. Eleanor didn't say a lot as it progressed. The women were all vocal supporters and all obviously close knit, and she was happy to let their conversation wash around her. Try as she might, though, she didn't feel like she belonged here, despite how welcoming they were.

It felt too…surreal.

Up until a couple of weeks ago, she was cattle crutching by

day and working on a commission for a playhouse in Adelaide at night. And now she was living in the city and rubbing shoulders with WAGS. If her and Bodie got married—her heart fluttered like butterfly wings at the thought of it—she'd *be* a WAG!

"What the hell are they doing?"

Eleanor tuned back into the game at Kathy Trimble's surprised enquiry. Ryder and Bodie appeared to be having words in the centre of the field.

Eleanor tensed. So did Juliet.

It was over as quickly as it had started though and they both relaxed a little, but Eleanor could hear the low buzz of speculation in the commentator's voices. And Griff, the only guy not wearing a spray jacket on the sidelines, his big mane of hair plastered to his head, didn't seem very happy, either.

Juliet patted her arm as the game played on. "I'm sorry." She kept her voice low. "He'll calm down. He just needs to beat his chest and be a Neanderthal for a bit."

Eleanor smiled. Being a little too acquainted with her brother and his inner caveman, she couldn't help it. She didn't really know her future sister-in-law well, but she liked her.

A lot.

The game progressed as if nothing had happened until Bodie fumbled a ball Ryder threw him. It slipped through his fingers initially, but he lunged and grabbed for it again, almost getting his hands on it before he fumbled it once more, and it fell from his grasp and was snatched by an opposition player.

It wasn't his first fumble. It wasn't *anyone's* first fumble. The ball had been slippery all night and holding on to it had been a nightmare.

But that didn't seem to matter. "Or maybe he won't," Juliet muttered, shaking her head as Ryder and Bodie bumped chests in the middle of the field, clearly yelling at each other, as the game played on.

Even across the distance and through the misty drizzle, Eleanor could see Griff was furious, storming up and down the sideline, gesticulating wildly at them.

The commentators were agog.

"What's up with them tonight?" It was Kathy again, but every eye in the box turned to her and Juliet.

Eleanor's heart sunk to her feet as her boyfriend and her brother pushed and yelled at each other, oblivious to their surroundings—the game, the crowd, their pissed-off coach. She couldn't hear what they were saying but it didn't look pretty.

"My brother is being an idiot."

"Yes," Juliet agreed. "He is."

That didn't really help. If anything, the WAGs' gazes became even more curious.

"Jesus." Val gaped at them. "They're going to get their asses benched."

"This is my fault," Eleanor whispered, half to herself, half to Juliet. This was the reason men had a ridiculous bro code—so stupid macho bullshit like this didn't happen.

"No. It's not. They're grown men acting like two-year-olds."

Eleanor knew she was right, but it didn't help her feel any less like Yoko. If she'd just been honest with Bodie that night back home, none of this would have unfolded.

But then she'd still be a frustrated virgin living a sensible life in the middle of nowhere.

She still wouldn't have *lived*.

Her heart thumped and her chest ached as she watched them bristle like two angry bears trying to mark their territory. Ryder shoved Bodie's shoulder and he stumbled back, almost falling over in the slippery grass. There was a collective gasp from the women as Eleanor's temper flared.

She loved her brother, but if he so much as laid a hand

on her man again, she was going to…punch him in the nose.

It seemed the camera men and the commentators had given up on the game in favour of the action going down in the middle of the field, too. So had the crowd.

Matilda frowned as Tanner tried to intervene. "What on earth are they fighting over?"

"Me."

Eleanor said it quietly, thought she'd whispered it actually, but given the weight of horrified silence, it was loud enough for everyone to hear. Loud enough for another round of speculative glances as she pressed her forehead against the cold glass and her hands to her belly.

No man had ever fought over her before. It was disturbingly hostile. Overwhelmingly masculine.

And wildly thrilling.

• • •

Griff kicked the open locker door in his way, and Bodie winced as the tinny crash echoed around the empty room.

Griffin King had been one of the best players the country had ever seen. Personal tragedy had hardened him from great into the stone cold legend he'd become, and when his body had finally dared to quit on him he'd become probably the best coach in the history of the game.

He was tough and uncompromising, but he got results. Every rugby player worth their salt wanted to play for the Smoke and if they managed to reach that lofty goal they pushed themselves harder than they'd ever done, just for him.

When he balled them out, it felt worse than disappointing their mothers. When he told them to jump, they asked how high. When he praised them, it felt like glories from heaven.

And when he spoke, they listened.

He whirled to face them. Even soaked to the skin and

his hair plastered to his head, he was a formidable guy. "One of you want to tell me what the *fuck* that was out there?" He pointed unnecessarily in the direction of the game that was still playing out in the middle.

He'd hauled their asses off, then left the two assistant coaches outside running the play while he dealt with this insurrection.

"It sure as shit better not have been about a fumbled ball."

Bodie didn't have to look at Ryder to know it was nothing to do with a slippery ball. But he was too steamed to answer. So apparently was Ryder.

"You do know you're on the same team, right?" Griff's head swivelled from one to the other. "The Sydney Smoke?" It swivelled again. "Blue and silver jerseys? The ones you're wearing?" He shot a long, hard glare at each of them. "We're the ones that are winning out there tonight, despite your combined monumental idiocy, in case either of you have taken your head out of your assess long enough to notice."

The locker door had swung open again, and Griff kicked it one more time for good measure.

"But we're not gonna with two of the *team* fucking about with a giant pissing match in the middle of the goddamn field."

Bodie shivered. He was wet to the bone, cooling rapidly, and epically fucked off at Ryder. But if he wanted warm hugs and hot chocolate, he wasn't going to get it from Coach.

"You both want to pull your dicks out now so we can measure them, or are you going to sort your shit out? Because neither of you are getting back on the field until you've kissed and made up. We have enough guys out there on that field wanting to bring us down without you two doing it from within."

He stormed out then, a slam of the locker room door

punctuating his departure.

Neither of them said anything for the longest time, just stood and stared at the door. Bodie wasn't sure what the hell had happened out there. Ryder had had a go earlier, but calling Bodie a *sister-fucking bastard* had made him see red—a whole tide of it flashing up and flaring in his head like an emergency beacon, goading him into confrontation.

But all Bodie felt now, apart from wet and cold, was hollow. He didn't want to fight with his best mate, he sure as shit didn't want to blow his rugby career for anyone, but he would for Eleanor. He'd take on the whole fucking world for her.

"I love her, man."

He didn't know where it had come from. He hadn't expected to say it. He didn't even know he'd felt it until this moment, but he couldn't have denied it even if the great Griffin King himself had demanded it.

It filled him up. Lifted him up. *Warmed* him up.

It was crazy but it was true.

The urge to run to the corporate box and tell her right now injected a restless energy into his muscles.

Ryder sighed. "Because of the baby?"

"No." Bodie shook his head emphatically. "*Not* because of the baby."

Eleanor had bewitched him from that first night. He hadn't been able to think of anything else in the three months he'd known her. He'd thought it'd had been the sex, the virginity thing. It was only now, wringing wet, staring down her brother in an empty locker room after practically coming to blows with him *during a game*, he knew this wasn't about his dick.

She didn't have him by the balls. She had him by the heart.

"Have you told her?"

Ryder's voice penetrated Bodie's internal dissection and he gave the ghost of a smile. "I only just found out myself."

"And how she's supposed to believe you, now?" Ryder's hostility was gone, replaced with a cutting matter-of-factness. "How's she ever going to know that you love her for her and not because of the baby?"

Bodie blinked, the racing of his thoughts halting abruptly. Well crap…he hadn't thought of that. He eased himself down onto the hard wooden bench between the rows of lockers, all that restless energy suddenly gone. Ryder joined him and they sat side by side, brooding gazes directed at the lockers as they dripped on the floor.

Is that what she'd think? That his love was some kind of *obligation* because of the baby? *Fuck that.* He loved her smarts and how she talked all prim and proper and how she blushed at every little thing and how damn talented she was and how her hair was always in a wild tangle and good God almighty, he loved her body to distraction.

But Ryder was right. With a baby in the mix, *would* she believe him? Would she believe *I love you* after two weeks of cohabitation? He could barely believe it himself. And Eleanor wasn't flighty or rash. She was considered. He'd been all set to get hitched in thirty days, but she'd wound him back. Hell, it had taken him a week to convince her to come to the game.

Blurting out *I love you* now could backfire. *Badly.* And he didn't want that. He wanted to be with her forever.

"I'll bide my time," Bodie said, coming out of his reverie to finally answer Ryder's question. "And I'll be here for her, always, *every* day. And maybe her brother not treating me like I troll the countryside for unsuspecting virgins to gobble up wouldn't hurt either."

"Yeah. Sorry about that. It's taken me a bit to get my head around it. Juliet told me to stop being a douche."

Bodie smiled. "Have I ever mentioned how much I like your fiancée?"

Ryder half laughed, half snorted, but then his face got really serious as he nailed Bodie with a protective big brother gaze. "If you fuck this up, man…if you hurt her…"

He didn't need to finish the sentence. Bodie understood the implications of failure. And not just on himself. But on their friendship. And the consequences for the team.

"I won't. I'm not going to fuck it up. And I won't hurt her."

And he meant it. He *loved* her. He just needed to keep it to himself for a while.

• • •

The following week, Eleanor was surprised to find herself at the trendy Mossman School of Design with Bodie. They were hosting a visiting fashion exhibition of Victorian clothing alongside student designs inspired by the era. It was in its last week and had been on Eleanor's list of things to do, but Bodie had surprised her by asking if he could accompany her.

And so here they were on a Thursday afternoon, wandering amongst the beautifully displayed designs, the down lights inside the glass cabinets complementing each piece perfectly. They were superbly done, so much so that Eleanor sometimes found it hard to tell the difference between the older clothes and the newer ones until she got up really close.

What was perhaps the most surprising was how interested Bodie was in it all. "This looks quite dapper."

Eleanor glanced over her shoulder at Bodie, who had stopped in front of a single cabinet housing a man's coat. She wandered over to him to admire it herself. "It's a frock coat."

"Frock coat doesn't sound very blokey."

She smiled at the tease in his voice but didn't take her eyes off the long formal coat. It was a new design from one of the students but made from a vintage pattern.

"It's *gorgeous.* The cut is exquisite and the velvet practically glows like a ruby." She almost pressed her nose to the case to examine it closer. "Look at the detail of the braiding on the cuffs and those perfect box pleats at the back. It's beautifully tailored."

Mr Darcy wouldn't be seen dead in it—too showy. It needed a man who didn't give a fig about what others thought of him.

She sighed, leaning into him. "I wish men still dressed like this. It's very dashing."

He chuckled all low near her ear, his hand sliding to her nape, his thumb rubbing seductively. "I love it when you talk Victorian." His lips buzzed her temple.

And in the middle of a very public place, she wanted him all over again. They'd already squeezed in a quick session when he'd got home from training before heading out to the exhibition, but his touch made her greedy.

He *had* created a monster!

His gaze wandered to her cleavage. "I hope you've gone the full nineteenth century under that dress."

Eleanor's nipples hardened as his warm breath brushed over her skin. She loved that he couldn't get enough of her old-fashioned lingerie. She especially loved the irony of it hiding her very modern, sparkly, twenty-first century-vagina.

"Not this time." The corners of his mouth turned down and she laughed. "It's okay, I have something else on I think you're going to *love*."

"Really?" His eyes lit up and heat flashed through her veins. "Tell me."

"No. It's a sur—"

"*Bodie*? Is that you?"

A shiver that had nothing to do with the brush of Bodie's fingers shot down Eleanor's neck. It intensified as Bodie stiffened and his hand dropped.

"Anna."

"It is you."

A tall, leggy blonde gave him an enthusiastic hug. She had hair that fell straight to the small of her back, a cute heart-shaped face, dazzling teeth, and two perfect dimples.

"Fancy meeting you here, of all places." She smiled at Eleanor and gave her a little eye roll. "Could barely manage to get him near any kind of clothes store when were together, let alone a clothing exhibition." She stuck out her hand. "Hi. I'm Anna."

Eleanor returned the shake as Bodie performed a perfunctory introduction. So, this was his ex. *God.* She was beautiful. The perfect mix of girl next door and goddess. Like Taylor Swift and Aphrodite had produced a love child.

Eleanor half expected to look up and see a permanent opening in the sky above her head streaming down glories.

Sure, Eleanor had Googled the other woman. She knew what Anna looked like. But her images just did not do her justice and she was…*here.* In Eleanor's face. Not staring back at her through the barrier of a computer screen.

The worse thing was Eleanor couldn't even hate the other woman. She was being perfectly polite and pleasant. Not bitchy or predatory or condescending. No trace of bitterness or trying to mark something that had once been hers with a sly touch or a flirty giggle.

She'd been inclusive, actually, drawing Eleanor into the conversation with smiles and eye contact as she complimented Bodie on the rugby season and asked after his parents. All while pretending not to notice Bodie's clipped replies.

God. What did *that* mean? Was it still hard to be around her over a year down the track? *Did he still love her?* Eleanor's heart pounded painfully at the thought.

"Anyway, I better go. I'm meeting Dad for a drink shortly." Bodie nodded, the rigidity of his body easing a little at the announcement. "Nice meeting you, Eleanor."

Eleanor smiled and nodded, unable to talk, feeling like a mute idiot as worry tightened her vocal chords.

"Say hi to your parents for me when you see them next, Bodie."

And then she swept away, her hair swinging in a perfect blonde swish.

Chapter Twelve

An hour later they were sitting in Bodie's car. The mood had been well and truly broken, and Eleanor had barely taken in the rest of the exhibition. Traffic choked the roads all around them as they made their way home. Bodie's silence was full and brooding in the confines of the car, and her stomach gurgled precariously.

She had two options. She could tough it out, take him home, show him her new underwear and let their hormones run wild, or she could do the sensible thing and attack this head-on. *Her hormones voted for the former.* But her brain knew this was too important to trust to a bunch of chemicals that had proved far too slutty for their own good these last couple of months.

"You're still in love with your ex."

It wasn't a question. It was a statement of what she thought could well be fact. One that her sinking heart had been whispering to her since Anna had swished off.

Bodie startled beside her. "*What?*" They were stopped in a line of traffic going nowhere, which was probably just as well.

Eleanor found some comfort in his surprise but she wasn't stopping until she knew it all. "She's very beautiful."

"So? What's that got to do with it?"

A part of Eleanor had wanted to hear him dispute it, but of course, it was undisputable. "I was thinking, you weren't acting like a man who'd moved on."

"Oh, I've moved on." His voice was deceptively neutral, but Eleanor didn't miss the way his knuckles whitened over the steering wheel.

"Really?" *Had* he moved on or was he just fooling himself? "Then why are you still so angry with her? You practically went rigid from the moment she spoke."

Bodie sighed and the tension in his shoulders eased. "I thought she might be…stalking me again. It took her a couple of months to adjust to it being over. Everywhere I went for a while after I called it off, she was mysteriously there."

"Oh."

The information mollified Eleanor slightly, but it was hard to imagine that tall, gorgeous, confident creature reduced to something needy and…pathetic. Unlike herself, who'd felt more and more needy and pathetic as she'd watched the ease with which Anna communicated.

Bodie inched forward in the traffic and braked again. He was in a pair of tan chinos and a button-down shirt that pulled across his incredible shoulders and exposed his tanned forearms.

He was beautiful, too. And Anna was perfect for him.

She'd let herself think these past couple of weeks they could make this work. That she could actually be with Bodie, be a family with him. But what was he doing with her when he could pull women like Anna?

She opened her mouth to ask him but shut it again, very much afraid of the answer as she spread her hand protectively against her belly.

"Eleanor, just say it. I can practically hear you thinking."

Eleanor shut her eyes and screwed up some courage. Country women didn't shy from hard truths or uncomfortable facts, and she wasn't going to start. But her pulse tap danced at her temples anyway. "I guess I'm confused why you'd settle for someone like me when you can have someone like her."

"Settle?" His brows beetled at her. "Is that what you think I'm doing?"

She couldn't work out from his tone if he was angry, surprised, or insulted. The truth was, she had no idea what the hell he was doing. She still didn't know why he'd chosen her that night back home.

"I…think you're trying to do the right thing."

"No."

He shook his head emphatically. He opened his mouth again like he was about to add something but shut it quickly, his fingers wrapping and unwrapping around the steering wheel. Eleanor didn't know what it was he'd been going to say, all she knew was that his quick, decisive denial had been a cool rush of air into her burning lungs.

"Anna is beautiful, I'll give you that, on the surface. But her priorities are all screwed up. Life's about money and social position for her. Just like my father. She's so…hard and tough underneath that veneer. And not in a resilient way, in an egocentric way."

"Did she change, or…?"

"No, she was always like that. I just chose to ignore it."

Eleanor almost asked why but stopped herself in time. Bodie was a guy. And Anna was a gorgeous woman. It didn't require a PhD to figure out—just eyes.

"I've known her most of my life. Our fathers were business associates. Everyone always kind of assumed we'd get together and we just…did. We both came from similar backgrounds, so we got each other. We were friends before we became lovers and our families were close and getting married at some stage seemed like the logical step…"

Eleanor didn't need a deck of tarot cards to hear the *but* coming.

"Then she cheated on me."

A gasp tumbled from Eleanor's mouth before she could haul it back. How could anyone cheat on a guy who was good and kind and doting? Not to mention fun to be around and thoughtful and honourable. *And* a genius in the bedroom? "I'm so sorry."

He shrugged. "She didn't see it as a big deal. I hadn't realised until that point that Anna had no romantic notions whatsoever about our relationship. She assumed that I was sleeping around, and having an open relationship made sense to her given that marriage was forever. As long as we were discreet. In fact, she pretty much took monogamy off the table."

Eleanor supposed someone who looked like Anna could do that with confidence. But Eleanor had marinated in romantic notions with every Heyer and Austen she'd read and she'd rather die a spinster than accept anything less than full fidelity and commitment.

"She genuinely couldn't see what the problem was. That my outrage at her betrayal was some kind of macho act that I'd get over. That I'd come to my senses when I saw the advantages of our union."

It sounded perfectly terrible to Eleanor.

"She saw our union as something practical. A mutually beneficial partnership. I did not."

Eleanor's heart just about swelled out of her mouth at Bodie's rejection of such a calculated union. "So you split?"

"Yes."

The definitive answer was pleasing. No wistful notes of

what if or *if only*. But still…

“It can’t have been easy.”

“It hurt for a while, turned me into a bit of cynic.” He shrugged. “Your brother was right. I spent a while there trying to soothe my battered ego with some women who *did* want more from me than a plus one at social events. But that got old and I stopped, decided to put my all into rugby, and then—”

Eleanor’s pulse leaped wildly as he reached for her hand and entwined his fingers with hers. Their surroundings melted away at his touch—there was no car cabin, no impatient traffic noises. Just him.

They could have been in a spaceship for all she cared.

“There was you. Talking about nineteenth-century hypnotists and looking like you wanted to melt into that potted palm.” He smiled. “You were so soft and warm and welcoming. Anna’s all hard edges and angles, her body *and* her personality. Her brain was always busy working out how to use situations and connections to her advantage. But you…” He kissed the back of her hand. “There was no agenda with you.”

Eleanor tried not to let his words go to her head. Or her heart. God knew they’d already crawled straight between her legs. “To be fair, there was the whole deflowering thing.”

He laughed. “Yes, but you didn’t go to the party specifically to lose your virginity, did you? You hadn’t checked out all our vital stats and our net worth and made a list of who to talk to and wrangled an introduction.”

“Of course not.” Was he crazy? The thought of talking to any of the beautiful people had left her in knots.

“No.” He nodded and smiled at her so gently it felt as if he was holding her heart in his hands. “You were just standing there and you were charming and captivating and the moment I saw you from across the room I knew I had to talk to you."

Eleanor's ribs felt too big for her chest. Lordy—the man had a way with words, snaking inside her and going straight to her head. Maybe she should be worried that he'd somehow subconsciously chosen her because she was the *opposite* of his ex. But he sounded well and truly shod of her and hell if she didn't want to throw her leg over him right now and thank him for making her feel like the only woman in the world.

Who knew sincerity was such an aphrodisiac?

"You want to hear about my underwear now?"

He laughed. "You know I do."

"I bought them this morning. They're Spider-Man inspired."

"Really?" Bodie's voice dropped, as did his gaze, lingering on her cleavage.

"The bra cups are like spider webs that stretch out over my boobs and just manage to hold everything in. *Lotta skin on display*. Maybe even some nipple."

"Jesus."

His nostrils flared and a corresponding flare zapped up Eleanor's spine. "And the pants have a spider web on the front and *bite me* stamped across the back."

He swallowed. "Sounds like an invitation I don't want to pass up."

"You really don't. You should hurry."

Eleanor grinned as Bodie surveyed the traffic with a frustrated eye and beeped his horn. "Out of my way. Man trying to get laid, people."

Miraculously, a clearing opened in the traffic, and Bodie didn't hesitate. Taking full advantage of the break, he accelerated away.

• • •

Eleanor had been nervous enough about meeting Bodie's parents, but that increased a hundredfold as they sat on the deck of their harbourside mansion a week later. Sparkling water and the arch of the Sydney Harbour Bridge were just visible through the trees.

They were seriously rich.

Ryder had told her a long time ago that his bestie had come from a wealthy family. And she'd Googled Bodie the day after the engagement party to find out his father, Conrad Webb, owned a mega successful financial services company. But views-of-the-harbour-bridge rich she hadn't expected.

Never in her life had she felt more like a country hick.

But it was his mother's birthday, and his father was hosting a family lunch in her honour. Plus, she was officially twelve weeks pregnant tomorrow, and Bodie figured it was as good a time as any for her to meet his parents.

Not to tell them about the baby—not just yet. They were telling her parents first, after the Smoke's game tomorrow. Today was more an introduction than anything.

And so here they were—all four of them—on a sunny Saturday, enduring a rather stilted affair, despite the stunning scenery. Bodie had never talked much about his parents and in this crushingly formal atmosphere she understood why. It was nothing like the raucous, talk-over-the-top-of-each-other carry on that generally punctuated a Davis family dinner.

His mother, Pamela, seemed nice, if a little strained, and was making an effort to converse with Eleanor, but his father had spoken to her just enough to find out she was Ryder's sister—a plus, she thought—and the daughter of a farmer.

Not a plus.

Conrad had said *farmer* in much the same way someone of his social standing might say *Kardashian*. Still, being dismissed was preferable to being hammered with questions like Bodie. About his investments and his endorsements and had he given any more thought to joining the company after his rugby career ended.

Bodie was clearly not comfortable with any of the questions, blocking and avoiding at every turn.

"Anna mentioned that she'd run into you at the Victorian fashion exhibition at the Mossman School of Design last week."

Eleanor stiffened at Pamela's enquiry and what was remaining of her appetite deserted her. She was sure his mother had only mentioned it to try and change the subject, but Eleanor already felt inferior enough in this company without bringing Anna into it.

"Yes," Bodie said, his jaw tight.

Conrad gave a harsh laugh, obviously finding the idea absurd. "What on earth were you looking at a bunch of old musty dresses for?"

A prickle of irritation burrowed into the back of Eleanor's neck. *Old musty dresses*? Conrad was *really* pushing his luck now.

"Eleanor's an expert on the Victorian era, particularly the fashion. She runs her own business making replica vintage clothing from the eighteen hundreds."

Conrad's eyebrows shot up. *Now* she had his attention. *Not* just a farmer's daughter.

Bodie took after his father in many ways. They had the same height and build, the same olive colouring. But there was a ruthless edge to Conrad that was unsettling. A sharpness that left her feeling like she'd had a dollar value put on her head.

"That's lovely," Pamela said, smiling kindly. "I can't sew a stitch. What's your business called?"

"Queen Victoria's Closet."

"What's its annual turnover?"

Eleanor blinked at the rapid-fire question from Conrad.

"Dad." The warning in Bodie's voice was loud and clear.

"What?" Conrad smiled, as if to show he was bearing no malice, but it didn't help. Not when it reminded her too much of a great white shark. "I'm just curious. From one businessperson to another."

Eleanor knew exactly what her annual turnover was, but she didn't think a paltry thirty thousand dollars would be enough to impress Conrad Webb.

"Oh it's just a small concern," she dismissed, her cheeks heating.

"So it's a *hobby?* Not a business?"

"That's enough, Dad."

Eleanor flinched at the steel in Bodie's voice. His mother's expression pinched slightly before she recovered to plaster a smile on her face and change the subject.

"Did you have a favourite dress in the exhibition?"

It took a moment for Eleanor to gather her thoughts. "My favourite garment wasn't a dress, actually. It was a man's frock coat, and it was divine. It was made by one of their students from a vintage pattern."

"Oh yes." Bodie squeezed her leg under the table as he nodded enthusiastically. She could have kissed him. "It was better than half that crap you see dudes wearing on catwalks."

His father stared incredulously at him, but Pamela ploughed on. "And that's the kind of thing you do?"

"Yes." Even to her own ears, Eleanor sounded stilted and she hated that the ease with which she usually slipped into her favourite subject was in tatters. "I make replica outfits from old patterns. Dresses mainly, but any item of clothing really."

There was no way Eleanor would tell them about the lingerie, but she was conscious of the pantaloons she was wearing beneath her A-line skirt. Or maybe that was just because of the heat of Bodie's palm on her thigh.

"So you'll be prancing around in frock coats, then?" Conrad jeered, his chin stuck out at an arrogant angle. "Can't see it myself."

"Oh I can."

The words slipped out before Eleanor could stop them, but she wasn't sorry. She had absolutely no problem seeing it. She'd been fantasizing about Bodie in that bloody frock coat for a week and had already made plans to make it for him over the coming months. Ideally, if they'd been going to have a wedding, she'd have made it for that, but no doubt there'd be some place he could wear it.

Bodie smiled at her, and it bubbled like a drug through her veins. She smiled back, suddenly giddy.

Conrad, on the other hand, looked like he was going to say more, but they were saved from it by two kitchen staff suddenly appearing with a couple of platters of Sydney rock oysters. Eleanor's stomach heaved at the sight of them, but she'd never been happier to see the slimy, snotty delicacy in her entire life.

• • •

After lunch, Conrad had asked Bodie for a private word and Bodie had reluctantly disappeared inside. Pamela invited her over to the railing, and they talked pleasantly about the history of the area and the house as they watched the Manly ferry head to Circular Quay.

Twenty minutes later the men were still gone, which made Eleanor nervous enough without holding onto her painfully stretched bladder. It was amazing how much she'd peed in the last twelve weeks! She asked Pamela for directions to the bathroom and hurried inside.

Washing up afterward, she inspected herself in the mirror. She'd ditched her regulation plastic claw and used pins to tame her hair today. She'd also chosen a blouse with a demure neckline and no corset underneath. The way Bodie looked at her when she wore one was not fit for polite company.

Still, she felt naked without it. Like a knight without armour, and she thanked God for her frilly-bummed pantaloons beneath her skirt, bolstering her confidence.

Not that it mattered what she wore—it didn't take a psychologist to know Conrad Webb was not much of an Eleanor fan. Even sadder, he didn't seem to be much of a Bodie fan, either. He hadn't asked Bodie a thing about rugby the entire time.

Eleanor would have thought that Conrad's giant ego would have lapped up his son's rugby god status. Instead, he treated it like it was an unfortunate diversion when Pamela had asked about it. An act of recalcitrance from a son whose one true path led to business, *not* sporting glory.

Heading back out to join Pamela again, she stopped abruptly in the corridor at the sound of her name. A door was cracked open. The fullness of her bladder had precluded all else on her way past, but she could see it now. And hear the conversation going on behind it.

She shouldn't eavesdrop. Wasn't there some old saying about people who listen in on others' conversations never hearing good of themselves? But she couldn't stop, either.

"What do you mean, you're going to *marry* her? You've known her for a few weeks!"

"I mean I'm going to get a license next week and in a month we're getting married."

Eleanor wanted to object. The deal was they were going to *talk* about getting a license next week. But given she was eavesdropping, she could hardly butt in. Not to mention the tiny trill of excitement that fluttered through her belly over Bodie's eagerness.

"You're going to marry a...seamstress? From buttfuck nowhere?" Eleanor couldn't see Conrad, but she was pretty sure he'd probably just spluttered that enquiry out with a bunch of spittle.

"Yes."

Bodie's voice was much lower than his father's, so Eleanor couldn't hear what inflection, if any, he'd used with that *yes*. Happy. Positive. Determined.

Resigned?

"Christ. She's up the duff, isn't she?"

"Dad."

"*Isn't* she?"

There was a pause for a beat or two and Eleanor held her breath, the thump of her heart so loud in her ears it must surely be reverberating around the hallway.

Say no. Tell him to...*go fuck himself.*

"What if she is?"

Groping for the wall beside her, Eleanor's breath left her lungs in a rush.

"I hope you're getting a paternity test."

Eleanor hadn't expected to hear congratulations. She expected anger and more bluster. But she hadn't expected this quick fire, calculated comeback. "I don't need one."

"Christ, son, don't be a fool. How many paternity suits are levelled against elite athletes? Not to mention rich ones with trust accounts."

A trust account? Bodie had a *trust account*?

"The baby is mine." Eleanor shut her eyes as the floor beneath her tilted. Bodie's decisive claim of paternity was the only bright spark in the ugly hue of this conversation.

"I thought they taught you to be smarter than that. I know I sure as shit did. I suppose you think you *love* her."

Eleanor's eyelids flew open. She needed to leave. *Now.* She ordered her feet to move. She *did not* want to hear this.

The contempt in Conrad's voice was bad enough.

But again, her feet refused to budge.

Bodie's stiff, "I'm not discussing this with you," lodged like a bullet in her heart.

What did *that* mean?

It was crazy to want him to say yes. It was ridiculous to think—to hope—he *could* be in love with her. This wasn't a Heyer novel. It was real life. And his father was correct, it was far too early for such…romantic folly. They'd only been together for a month.

So why did it hurt so much he'd *not* said it?

Why?

Because he'd dismissed it so quickly? Like it hadn't even entered his head?

That thought was like a fist to her throat and she hurried away, wishing she'd never stopped to eavesdrop at all.

Chapter Thirteen

"You're not going to join the family business after your rugby career ends, are you?"

Bodie was startled out of his reverie by the question. They were driving home from his parents' house, the *conversation* with his father still playing heavily on his mind. He maintained a relationship with his father for his mother's sake, but it was getting harder and harder to stay civil.

Hell, if he hadn't wanted to knock his father's flashy white veneers down his neck as he'd tried to cast doubt on the paternity of his baby.

"Not even if I was penniless."

She visibly relaxed, and so did he. She'd been quiet—more so than usual—during the meal and had practically dragged him to the car when he'd suggested it was time to leave.

"I'm sorry about my father." He gave a dismissive shrug. It was what it was. If it had been up to Bodie, he'd have kept Eleanor away from him for much, much longer. But with their marriage hopefully imminent, it was inevitable that it would be sooner rather than later.

"Has he always been so…full on?"

Bodie almost laughed out loud at her polite euphemism for overbearing. "Yes." It pained Bodie to admit it but it was true. "He comes from old money. Generations of private schools breeding ruthless businessmen. Everything is an acquisition or a merger to him. He doesn't know anything else."

"I'd have thought old money would be into the whole rugby scene, though?" The sport was, after all, firmly entrenched in the private school culture.

Bodie snorted. "No. He had a particular career path in mind for his son and heir and it didn't involve being sidetracked by something as frivolous as sport."

"Yes, but…you were obviously really good at it?"

There was an incredulity in her voice that only someone who has come from a large, loving extended family could affect.

The kind of family he wanted for his baby.

"It didn't matter. He always discouraged it. He never came and saw me play as a kid. In fact, he's rarely seen me play with the Smoke, unless he has some clients he wants to impress with free entry to his corporate box."

"I'm sorry."

Her voice trembled with empathy. If he wasn't driving he'd lean right over and kiss that troubled little V between her brows. He was used to his old man's crap but it had clearly shaken Eleanor.

"I do have a lot to thank him for," Bodie admitted. "I get my drive to win, my competitive streak from him. Getting ahead in this sport, getting to an elite level, requires a killer instinct, and I learned it from the best."

She nodded and he knew she understood. Her brother might be all laid-back-cowboy on the surface, but under it all he was as focused on his career as the rest of the team.

"I'm my father's son." Frankly that scared the bejesus out of him.

"No." She shook her head vehemently. "You're not like him, you know why? Because you play on a team. You've learned the people around you make you stronger, and you need to trust them to have your back just as you have theirs. Business is a solo sport, and your father's learned not to trust anyone. That doesn't make him strong. It makes him foolish."

Bodie blinked. She really *hadn't* liked his father.

"I don't want to..." He'd spoken before the thought had fully formed, and he stumbled over it now as he realised he was about to express his deepest fear.

"What?"

He glanced at her briefly, at the unhappy set of her mouth. It seemed their visit with his parents had unsettled her as much as it had unsettled him. "I don't want to be the kind of father he was."

Bodie hadn't thought too much about it before today, but he was now. Standing in his father's office, the walls closing in on him, he'd known he didn't want anything like this for his kid.

"So don't be."

His forehead furrowed at her slightly terse reply. She was more tense than he'd realised. "You're right...it's just rugby season is intense. It takes over my life. It requires all my focus."

"There's a difference between focused and blinkered, Bodie."

"What if I can't tell the difference?" A cramp knotted just under his sternum. That was his biggest worry, *unintentionally* turning into his dad.

She smiled but it seemed forced. "That's what I'm for."

Man, he liked the sound of that. But a couple of hours in his father's company had really messed with his head. And hers, too, if her demeanour was anything to go by. He opened his mouth to ask her if she was okay, but she leaned forward to turn the radio up as Ed Sheeran crooned *Perfect* and the unease that something was wrong faded away as she hummed along to the lyrics.

Eleanor was standing in front of the open fridge sucking out of a can of whipped cream when Bodie found her.

"Here you are."

He'd stripped off to all but his underwear and smooshed the front of his body up against the back of hers, his dick already semi hard. Sliding a hand onto her jaw, he turned her face and kissed her, stealing some of the sweet, fluffy goodness from her mouth as Eleanor tried to laugh, breathe, swallow, and kiss him back at the same time.

She wished like hell they could stay here forever in his apartment and never have to face the world and its judgement again. Everything felt like it was going to be okay inside these four walls.

"Mmm." He licked his lips as he broke off the kiss. "I thought you were coming straight up."

"I barely ate at your parents'. I'm starving." She'd been too nervous to start with, then too bloody sick to her stomach after *that* overheard conversation.

"It's okay." His hands dropped to her waist, pulling her blouse out of her skirt. "I can help you with that."

He grabbed the bottom of her shirt on either side of the row of central buttons and ripped upward. The hard plastic discs pinged off the fridge, half landing *inside* the fridge, the other half scattered on the floor at their feet.

"Bodie," Eleanor half protested, half laughed. "How is that helping?" But he was already onto the second part of his plan, whipping the can out of her hands, shoving the nozzle between her cleavage and depressing the pump.

She yelped as cold cream filled the V between her breasts. Then he was turning her in his arms and dipping his head to lick off every last morsel, groaning at the taste. His cock pressed into the juncture of her thighs and Eleanor arched her back, fully gone on the way he made her body feel.

At least they had this, right? He might not love her but they had a physical compatibility that was off the charts. And they liked each other and had fun. Marriages had been based on worse, right?

He finally lifted his head from her cleavage. "That'll teach you for not being naked already."

Eleanor eased back, glancing at his underwear. His rock hard cock stretched the fabric, busting to get out. "*You're* not naked."

"That's because I was too impatient to get my hands on you."

"That looks painful." She plucked at the band of his underwear, pulling it out, very satisfied at what she found. "Think it could do with something to soothe it."

Bodie nodded, barely suppressing a smile. "I think you're right."

She smiled at him as she grabbed the can of cream out of his hands, shoved the nozzle in his pants and squirted.

"*Fuck* that's freezing."

He snatched for the can but Eleanor was faster this time, dropping it on the floor and kicking it across the polished concrete. She quirked an eyebrow at him. "That'll teach *you* not to be naked already."

He narrowed his eyes. "You better be prepared to clean that up, woman."

"Absolutely."

Eleanor salivated at the thought as she sunk to her knees,

one hand pushing the fridge door shut, the other easing his underwear off his hips. His cock sprang from the confines of his clothes and even covered in whipped cream it was impressively masculine.

She shut her eyes as her tongue swiped at the sweet, fluffy confection coating his dick, licking it off then sucking him clean, revelling in the deep timbre of his groans and the way his hands slid into her hair. But it wasn't enough. She needed him *inside* her. *Part* of her. Bodie's father had asked him today if he loved her and he'd deflected and that had hurt, so what she needed right now was to be as close to him as she could, to negate the things his father had said, to know this was more than Bodie being trapped or doing the honourable thing.

He seemed to be thinking the same thing, reaching for her as she slid her mouth from him.

"I want to be inside you," he said and it couldn't have been more perfect.

Eleanor went willingly, wrapping her legs around his waist, moaning against his mouth as she kissed him and murmuring her approval as he slid her onto the kitchen bench and claimed the space between her legs, spreading them wide with his hips. He pushed up her skirt, one hand skimming the fine linen of her pantaloons, the other guiding his cock to the open seam.

She moaned, her heart skipping crazily as his cock slipped through the easy access and slid through the slick folds of her sex, finding the hot, wet heart of her. And then she titled her pelvis just right as he pushed in and he was deep inside her, sunk to the hilt.

He followed that with a slow, sexy grind. Easy, deep glides. *So deep,* pressing in and holding before a long, lazy withdrawal. And a lot of hot, wet kissing as his fingers found the swollen knot of nerves between her legs, inching

Eleanor closer and closer, inching him closer and closer. Heat building, sweat building, trembles building until she cried out, clamping around him tight, undulating along the length of him, milking him with the rigors of her orgasm, yanking him into the rigors of his, twisting through the rapture, holding one another through the chaos.

Holding one another through the rise and the fall and the slow, hazy drift back to earth.

"Christ." He panted into her neck. "I think we just keep getting better and better."

Yes. He knew how to love her with his body and that was better than a lot of people got. A satisfied kind of laugh rumbled in her throat. "Amen to that."

He smiled and pulled back slightly to study her. "Sorry, we seem to make a habit out of not making it to the bed."

Eleanor opened her eyes, her head lolling a little. "It's fine." Here, like this, with him, she didn't need anything else. A bed included. "But you might have to carry me up the stairs because the only thing I can feel at the moment is my vagina, and I don't think it's up to the job."

He laughed this time. "Never underestimate your vagina. That thing is fucking amazing."

She deliberately tightened around him, still hard inside her, and he growled low in his throat, kissing her quick. "Hold on."

Bodie grabbed her ass as he slid her off the counter, his dick still rammed to the hilt. Eleanor protested to be put down, but he just kept walking and she held on tight, locking her ankles around his waist. "I was only joking. You can't carry me up the stairs. I'm too heavy."

He snorted. "You're a lightweight compared to what I can handle."

"You could fall and break something. Your leg. Or your penis." She met his gaze. "That's a thing, you know. I read about it. "

He laughed. "Yeah, well, in that case I expect you to give it mouth to mouth resuscitation."

He hit the stairs and powered up them like he was Rocky. "I think I just swooned," she whispered in his ear as he stepped into the bedroom. He kissed her then and things got a little hazy as her libido roared back to life.

"Hold that thought." She broke off and squirmed to be let down. "Need the bathroom."

"Of course you do." He shook his head, grinning at her as he eased her down, playfully swatting her ass. "Hurry."

She did hurry but what she discovered when she sat on the toilet brought everything to a screeching halt. Oh God.

"*Bodie.*"

There must have been something in her voice because he was in the bathroom doorway within seconds. "What's wrong?"

"I'm bleeding."

• • •

Eleanor held her breath as the doctor lubed up her abdomen. Bodie, tense beside her, tightened his grip on her hand.

"Okay, let see what we got."

The female doctor smiled at them sympathetically. She was young, maybe thirty, and had been enormously supportive and encouraging. Eleanor had only had some spotting and nothing further. It was apparently quite common and with the absence of any cramping or abdominal pain the doctor was confident it would be okay.

Bodie had been amazing. They'd been at the hospital in twenty minutes, and he hadn't left her side, telling her it was going to be okay. But he was worried, and she could tell he was still blaming himself.

He'd castigated himself out loud multiple times on their trip to the hospital. For the bench top, for the angle of his thrust, for going so deep and staying there so long.

For generally being a *horny douchebag.*

The doctor had assured him that cervixes were much stronger than that, *built to take a real pounding* she'd joked, but Eleanor could tell Bodie wasn't convinced.

The ultrasound probe slid through the gel and the picture on the screen was fuzzy and indistinct as she moved it around to position it correctly. A wave of nausea flashed through Eleanor's abdomen.

When she'd first done those tests, she'd entertained the notion of something like this happening—miscarriage was common, after all. She certainly hadn't been adverse to it as a solution to her predicament, and it had seemed a far easier option than actively doing something about it.

And it would be an easy out for Bodie—if he wanted it—if there was no heartbeat.

I'm not discussing this with you.

The cryptic words he'd spoken to his father earlier today brewed like a batch of off prawns in her gut. There'd be no obligation if this was to end tonight. He could put this behind him and get on with his life.

They both could.

But there was a connection to the fragile little life inside her she couldn't deny. She wasn't sure when it had grown so strong but Eleanor felt it acutely now as the baby flickered on the screen. *She* wanted it whether he did or not. *Whether he loved her or not.*

It was as much a part of her as her own heartbeat, as the breath in her lungs. And she couldn't bear the thought that the baby might have ceased to exist.

But there it was on the screen, safe inside the amniotic sac. A human-looking jelly bean, a pulsing blip blinking away like the mothership at the centre. The doctor tapped a button and the cubicle filled with the rapid *whop whop whop* of a tiny heartbeat.

She smiled at them. "Isn't that a beautiful sound?"

Relief poured like cool water through Eleanor's veins as Bodie stood and leaned in closer to the screen.

"It's fine?" His voice was a strained mix of hope and desperation.

"It's fine," the doctor confirmed. "Heart rate one hundred and forty-three. Perfect."

He sat then, or maybe collapsed was a better word for it, pressing his forehead to her hand, his shoulders heaving as he breathed in and out, slow and deep. "The baby's fine," Bodie said, lifting his head and capturing her gaze.

"Yes." Eleanor's heart squeezed hard as Bodie turned to stare at the screen again. He seemed as relieved as she did, and a flood of emotion rushed in.

Oh Lordy…

Eleanor shut her eyes against the sure and sudden knowledge pushing its way into existence. She didn't just love this tiny life blinking away inside her, she loved the man who had given it to her.

She was in love with Bodie Webb.

She hadn't let herself think in those terms these past four weeks—past few months, actually. In fact, she'd resolutely pushed away anything that had resembled an examination of her feelings. She was pregnant—*to Bodie*—how *could* she trust the veracity of her emotions?

She'd had to make this about the baby. Not the baby's father.

Because she knew herself too well. She knew she was prone to flights of fancy. That it would be easy to get swept away in the romance of their situation—a forced marriage to legitimize a pregnancy. *How very Victorian*. It was like rain to her parched romantic soul.

So she'd been ruthless in her plan to get to know Bodie without falling in love with him. To ignore the temptation of his marriage proposal and think and act logically over the situation.

But who had she been kidding? She'd fallen in love with him the night he'd taken her virginity and it was as clear to her now as the tiny blinking heartbeat on the screen.

So much for logic.

Her heart cracked wide open and she could no more have denied her feelings than denied her next breath. She'd absolutely marry him—whatever his feelings—and make him so damn happy and satisfied he couldn't help but fall in love with her, too.

They'd be a family. Bodie, her, and the baby.

Unshed tears shone in Bodie's eyes as he tore them off the screen and looked at her. "That's our baby."

A lump lodged in her throat. "Yes."

"He's beautiful."

Eleanor laughed. She had no idea what the sex was. Maybe the doctor could tell? It wasn't important. She loved him, that's what was important, and the baby could be whatever the hell sex he wanted in this moment. "He is."

• • •

It was seven by the time they arrived home again and Bodie insisted she go to bed. "To Netflix and chill. And no that is *not* code for sex. We're not having sex until after the baby is born."

Eleanor laughed as she stripped off to just the pair of plain, white boy leg undies she'd worn to the hospital. "Yeah, right." She crawled under the sheets and sighed at the bliss of a familiar bed. It had been a long day—lunch with his parents seemed like a very long time ago.

"I mean it," he insisted, also stripping down to his underwear.

"The doctor said the sex had nothing to do with it."

"Maybe." He slid in beside her. "But tonight scared the bejesus out of me. I'm not going through that again."

"Not even if I get some more vagazzling?" The last jewels had fallen off a week ago.

"Not even."

Eleanor shrugged nonchalantly. "Okay. Whatever you want."

He narrowed his eyes at her. "I'm not kidding around."

"I know." But she grinned. God, he was so earnest, and her heart just about burst out of her chest.

It was going to be so much fun dissuading him.

"Seriously."

She kissed his shoulder as she snuggled into him, sliding her hand over the steady thump in the centre of his chest. "Have you forgotten my powers are on the rise?"

He groaned and Eleanor could feel it reverberate through her palm. "You're going to make it difficult, aren't you?"

She laughed as she slid her hand down his abdomen. "Count on it."

He muttered something under his breath as he caught her hand and plonked it firmly back where it had come from, his big hand on top to keep it there. She laughed some more and they settled down to watch a couple of episodes of the latest series.

• • •

She wasn't sure what time it was when she woke or what had woken her but something had. Something wasn't right. The luminous digits on the bedside clock told her it was almost two. Bodie's big warm body was spooning her from behind, his hand heavy where it rested low on her abdomen.

But it wasn't the weight that was causing the heaviness, she realised. It was internal, not external. A churning sensation, a low dragging sensation in her belly like a period pain.

A really bad period pain.

And there was more. She felt wet and despite her woolly brain, Eleanor automatically reached down, her pulse an unsteady thump in her ears. It was wet alright, and even in the dark of the room, she could see the blood on her hand as she pulled it from between her legs.

It was a *lot* of blood.

A sob escaped her throat as she stared at it, the terrible realization hitting her. "*Bodie.*"

Chapter Fourteen

They were back home again from the hospital at midday the next day. Neither of them would ever be the same people. The cavernous space of Bodie's apartment seemed even emptier to Eleanor, which was stupid. It wasn't like something the size of a golf ball that wasn't even born yet could ever have filled it up.

But the emptiness was inside her, too, and yawned between them, pushing them apart.

"Are you okay?" Bodie asked, hovering near her elbow.

He'd asked her that approximately every ten minutes since two this morning.

"Yes." But she wasn't. She was far from okay.

"Why don't you…go to bed, and I'll bring you a cup of tea."

Eleanor shook her head. "I want a shower."

"Okay." He slid a hand onto her hip. "I'll help you."

"I don't need help."

She hadn't meant to snap at him. Could have bitten her tongue off in the next instant, but she didn't want him to touch her. She felt dirty and exhausted and a failure, and she was so close to bursting into tears—tears she'd kept in check all night and day—she couldn't bear his kindness.

She wanted nothing more than to throw herself into his arms and cry. And if they'd been a traditional couple, if they'd done this the right way round, if she was sure of how he felt about her, she could have. She *would* have.

But they weren't, and the last thing she wanted was his pity hugs, wondering if he had one eye on the door.

She turned away, swaying as the room tilted, and he grabbed her elbow. "Let go," she grouched as she yanked her arm out of his grip.

"Fuck, Eleanor. You're pale as a ghost…and there was *so much blood.*" He shoved his hand through her hair. "You look like you're about to fall down. I'm not letting you go in the shower alone."

She eyed him. He was pale, too, beneath the olive hue of his skin, and she tried to remember that he'd been through the same thing she'd just been through. That he'd seen the blood flooding onto the crisp, white hospital sheets as well. The doctor had told her it seemed more than it actually was, but it had frightened him.

Maybe it had been worse for him because he hadn't been able to do a damn thing. *Not even take her pain.* She'd felt his helplessness as a tangible force brooding and frustrated beside her, but she'd been too caught up in her own misery to acknowledge his.

"Fine."

She was too tired to argue as she turned away from him, aware of him close behind as she walked, hovering closer still as she slogged up the stairs she normally took two at a time. He followed her to the en suite and turned on the shower for her as she shucked off her clothes, then sat on the edge of the bath, head in his hands as she turned the heat and the pressure up as hot and as hard as she could bear.

The water drummed against her skin, washing away more than the blood. Washing away the crisp feel of starched hospital sheets, the soft touch of well-meaning nurses, and the stench of antiseptic which would forever remind her of the night she'd lost her baby.

A sob rose in her throat and she pushed it down, reaching for the soap, rubbing it over her skin, wishing it was a brush so she could scrub. *Scrub hard.* Scrub until she was as raw on the outside as she was on the inside.

Eleanor's skin was red from the heat, her cheeks flushed, her head swimming when she finally shut off the taps. Bodie was there at the shower door, holding up an unfolded towel, and she stepped straight into it, pressing her forehead to his chest as he wrapped her up in it.

He held her then, his lips at her temple, and she had to bite down on the inside of her cheek to stop from crying.

"You tired?"

She nodded. She hadn't slept all night. Neither had he. Pain, anxiety, grief had kept them both awake during the hours their baby had slipped from her body. She was lucky, she supposed, that the miscarriage had been straightforward in a medical sense. There'd been blood and cramping, but she'd passed the sac as a whole—no need for an operation or admission.

The severe pain had stopped almost immediately and the bleeding had settled dramatically.

"Come on, honey." He pressed a soft kiss to her temple. "Let's get you to bed."

Her energy completely sapped now, Eleanor just managed to dress while Bodie changed the sheets. She sank into them a minute later, her eyes already closing, seeking the restorative powers of sleep and the dark oblivion of unconsciousness.

She woke some time later, her throat raw and scratchy. It was dark and Bodie was stepping into his pyjamas. Unlike last night, she wasn't disorientated, she remembered *everything.*

Immediately.

In full, terrible Technicolor detail. Red and grey and black. Blood and pain and grief.

"Sorry, I didn't mean to wake you," he whispered. "How are you feeling?"

"What time is it?"

"It's six thirty."

Eleanor frowned at Bodie's pyjamas as the cloak of grief lifted and the real world intruded. "Shouldn't you be at Henley?" With everything that had happened in the last twenty-four hours, his game had slipped her mind but it was front and centre now.

The Smoke were going gangbusters and a win tonight would cement their ranking in the top four.

"I'm not playing."

"*What?*" Eleanor sat up. "No, Bodie. You *have* to play. I'm fine."

He shook his head, tiredness etched into every line of his face. He looked awful. His designer stubble was more haggard then sexy and his hair appeared to have been the victim of much finger combing.

"You just had a miscarriage. I'm not leaving you, Eleanor."

The rawness at the back of her throat grew bigger. His words shot rays of sunshine into the heavy darkness weighing her down. But he didn't have to do any of this anymore and there was something bigger at stake. "You have to. Griff will have your guts for garters."

"I've rung Griff. He might be a hard-ass, but he does

have a heart in there somewhere. I also told Ryder. He rang before to check if everything was okay and…he's going to know soon enough anyway."

Eleanor didn't care. She *did* care about Bodie committing career suicide. She knew how important his career was and she did not want him to jeopardise it for her sake. "I don't care if Griff's fine with it. You should still go." She threw a quick glance at the clock. "If you hurry you can make it in time for kickoff."

"No."

"Bodie." She fixed him with a glare. "There's nothing you can do here anyway."

His brows drew together. "Damn it, Eleanor. It was my baby, too." His eyes blazed down at her. "I don't feel like playing fucking football tonight."

Eleanor blinked at the raw emotion in his voice. It sounded like the back of her throat felt. Tight and achy and ragged. She'd been so wrapped up in her own loss, she hadn't given a lot of thought to his.

That the baby had been as real to him as it had to her.

"I just want to lay in bed with you and hold you and feel sorry for us for a bit."

A lump swelled in Eleanor's throat, making it rawer still. She needed the same. She shouldn't. The baby was gone and with it the reasons why Bodie was with her. But for now, she'd very much like to lie with Bodie and wallow in their misery.

"I'm sorry." She pulled back the covers beside her. "Get in."

He slid in, rolling them onto their sides, one big arm clamping across her belly as he dragged her back into the hardness of his chest, spooning her. Eleanor couldn't stop the fresh rise of emotion prickling at her nose, burning at her tear ducts, clawing at her throat.

She felt warm and safe and loved and it *slayed* her that

she'd never feel this again. "It's my fault," she whispered on a sob.

"No." His warm breath was a gentle caress on her nape. "It was nobody's fault."

Eleanor shut her eyes tight and screwed up her nose trying to hold back the tears. "In the beginning I thought a miscarriage—" Her voice broke. "It seemed like a solution to..."

"Shhh." He kissed her neck. "It's okay."

But it wasn't. She cried then. Silently at first, trying to hold it inside, her lungs bursting, her muscles trembling with the effort.

His lips brushed her nape, warm and gentle. "Let it go, honey."

A sob slipped from between her lips. Then another. Then the dam wall burst, and she lay broken and helpless in his arms, her body shaking, wracked with grief and guilt and loss. And he held her throughout, whispering and crooning. Telling her it was no one's fault, telling her she was strong and brave, telling her he was in awe of her.

Telling her it would all be okay.

It was the last thing she heard before she fell asleep and for those crazy moments between consciousness and oblivion, she actually believed him.

• • •

Eleanor was awake at dawn. She stared into the darkness, her gaze locked on the weak light she could just make out through the massive windows. Her eyes were gritty, her mouth dry, her limbs as heavy as wet blankets. There was a low, dull ache at her temples to match the low, dull ache in her chest.

She was utterly exhausted. Wrung out despite how long she'd slept.

Bodie was still snuggled around her, but there was an alertness to his body that told her he was also awake.

"You should go to training." Her voice was croaky and talking felt like a dagger in her throat.

His arm tightened around her. "No." His voice sounded as rough as hers.

"I want you to go." Hot tears stung her eyes but she blinked them back.

"I'm not going to leave you."

Eleanor took a deep breath and turned in his arms until she was lying on her side facing him. He looked as tired as she felt, and her aching heart swelled with how much she loved him. She slid a hand onto his whiskery jaw, wishing they could stay like this forever, cocooned in this bed with him looking at her like he meant what he'd just said.

But she couldn't buy into something like that. She was too emotionally vulnerable at the moment with her womb empty and her heart broken. She may be a romantic, but she'd always come in a practical wrapper.

"You've already missed a game." Who had even won the damn thing? "I don't think you should try Griff's patience anymore."

"Griff will be fine." His quick, gruff denial made her heart lift a little, but his follow-up had it plunging again. "My place is here with you."

Eleanor felt each word as a body blow, and she fought hard not to crumple into a ball. *Oh God.* She was some kind of *duty* to him now. The miscarriage should have freed him, but instead he was going to hold on harder because it was his *place.*

She *loved* him and he was doing what was *expected.*

She forced her features into a mask of neutrality even as the wound in the centre of her chest widened. "Life has to go on."

He stared at her for long moments, then shook his head. "Fuck that." He rolled away, climbing out of the bed, regarding her for a beat or two. His face was a clash of emotions. "We can still get married."

The urge to laugh hysterically bubbled in her chest and Eleanor made a kind of a gurgling noise as she suppressed it. Talk about adding insult to injury. She hadn't thought she could feel any worse—she'd been wrong.

Get married? Was he *trying* to hurt her? Did he honestly think it made things better? "What?"

The room was growing light enough for Eleanor to see the clench of his jaw. "I can go and get a marriage license application today and in thirty days we can go to the town hall and be married. Just like we'd planned."

Her chest turned to ice. She couldn't believe what she was hearing. A quickie marriage, as much as it had killed off a little of her romantic soul, had made sense a few weeks ago, but now? "There's no reason to get married now."

"No reason?" He glowered down at her. "I love you. Isn't that enough reason?"

Eleanor gaped at him. She'd spent a lot of time fantasising about this moment. Both in a general sense throughout her life and in a more specific sense in relation to Bodie.

This was *not* how it was supposed to go down.

There was no grand gesture, no music, no flowers. No beautiful scenery. Just a man in his underwear glowering at her as he threw down the three words she'd most wanted to hear from him. Like they were some kind of consolation for what had been probably the worst night of her life.

Her stupid, traitorous, romantic heart leaped at them regardless. It didn't care what bow they came wrapped in, or if there was a bow at all. But, *God*...she couldn't handle this. Her stomach was knotted, her emotions pitched and rolled inside her until she thought she might throw up.

It was everything she'd wanted. But it was all wrong.

"Since when?" she asked. How was she supposed to believe he loved her? *Loved* her. When the whole basis of their relationship had been the baby?

A baby that no longer existed?

The horrible knowledge was like hot talons sinking into her chest. Eleanor rolled out of bed. She couldn't have this conversation with him while he was towering over her. She needed to be strong to separate the raw emotions from reality. And her grandmother had taught her that strong women stood on their own two feet.

"I've known since that night Ryder and I argued on the field."

God. He sounded so sincere, and she desperately wanted to believe him. But why hadn't he said anything to her, then? Why not tell his father he loved her the other day, if it was indeed the case? "Damn it, Bodie. How am I supposed to believe that now?"

"Hell, Eleanor…" He rubbed a hand over his jaw. "I *couldn't* tell you then. I didn't want you to think I was only saying it because you were pregnant. I didn't want you to think it was because of the baby."

"But telling me after I *miscarried* our baby is okay? Are you trying to tell me that confessing your love now *isn't* about the baby? Isn't some consolation prize? Some *pity* statement because we're both so…" Eleanor hunted around for a description worthy of Austen to describe their turmoil but ultimately it was Bodie's vocabulary that inspired. "*Fucked up* by it?"

"No." He stalked toward her. "It's not like that, Eleanor. I love you. What's happened doesn't change that. *Nothing's* changed."

"How can you say that, Bodie?" A sob Eleanor didn't even know had been building in her chest escaped. "Everything's changed."

He slid his hands onto her upper arms. "Not for me."

Eleanor *wanted* to believe him. With all her heart she wanted to believe him. But she'd be a fool to let her romantic notions get in the way of common sense. Their emotions were raw and running high. She couldn't accept his words of love. She certainly couldn't accept his marriage proposal when they were both reeling from what had happened.

It was too big and too much and too soon. They needed to take a breath. Not be making major life decisions mired in grief. Those things needed to be decided with clear heads.

"I can't, Bodie." She shook off his hands and brushed past him. "I can't think properly at the moment. I can't think beyond losing the baby. I can't…" She tunnelled her fingers into her hair. "My brain, my *heart*, is still back in the hospital."

He sighed, his shoulders slumping as he nodded in acknowledgement. "I'm sorry." He crossed the distance between them and pulled her in for a long hug. Eleanor shut her eyes. It felt so right here in his arms, she never wanted to move.

But…

"Please," she murmured, drawing strength from the steady thump of his heart, "just go to training. I've got enough whirling around in my head without stressing about you damaging your career."

He was damn lucky to have the distraction. She'd give anything for a major sewing project or a big muster right now.

"Okay." He kissed the top of her head. "If that's what you want."

"It is."

He pulled away slightly, his gaze meeting hers. "We'll talk some more when I get home."

Eleanor nodded. But deep down she knew she needed to go home to Bungindally.

• • •

Waiting for Bodie to return after training was excruciating. She'd contemplated just skipping out and leaving him a note. But she couldn't do that. Not again. Not after all they'd been through. He deserved a face-to-face explanation.

Her ticket was booked. Her bags were packed. The freight company she'd spoken to had already come and boxed up her fabric and other purchases from the last four weeks and taken them away.

All that was left was to wait for Bodie.

And hold herself together.

He was home promptly at twelve thirty, obviously deciding to ditch a post-training shower to get home as soon as possible. He was sweaty, his shirt plastered to his chest, his hair wet with perspiration as he stepped through the heavy doors. There was worry in his eyes as they met hers but he smiled and she almost lost the tight rein she had on herself.

His smile faded as his gaze took in her bags sitting just inside the door. "Where are you going?" His words were clipped, his jaw tight.

"I've booked a flight home."

He shook his head. "Don't do this Eleanor. *Please*."

The inflection on please almost undid her. "I need some time, Bodie."

"Take it." He crossed to her quickly, sliding his hands onto her arms like he did this morning, his gaze boring into hers. "Have it. Have as much as you like, just don't *leave me*."

Her belly twisted hard. *This wasn't fair.* He was saying all the right things, and he was so damn tempting. Even with everything her body had been through, it yearned for him on a primal level.

"You want me to beg?" He fell to his knees, his hands gathering hers close, holding them. "I'm not too proud to beg."

"Don't." She shut her eyes against the sight tearing her in two. Her pulsed tripped. "Get up, Bodie."

He shook his head vehemently. "I love you, Eleanor."

It should have been the right thing to say—to hear—but it was the one thing that hardened her heart. She shook her hands free of his and walked away, staring unseeingly out the lovely floor-to-ceiling windows she loved so much. "You don't *know* me."

Not really. Not who she was deep down. If he did, he'd not have told her he loved her in a moment of high emotion. He'd not have repeated his offer of a quickie marriage in a town hall.

"I *know* you." His desolate voice came from behind her. "You're funny and sexy and quirky and smart and you have your own business. And I took you out of your comfort zone, and you didn't bitch or complain. You didn't withdraw or wither. You bloomed."

He was right. She had bloomed. Under his blatant attraction she was more confident. More comfortable in her skin. But deep down she was still the nerdy girl with her head stuck in a romance novel spinning her dreams of a happily ever after.

If he'd really known her, he'd *know* her romantic soul. He'd know she wanted the fairytale. The courtship, the proposal, asking her father's permission, the grand wedding.

Because she did. She wanted them with him. And it wasn't just about the romance. It was about the shy little wallflower inside her who still found it hard to believe that a guy like Bodie could love a woman like her.

"And you're so fucking *brave*. What you went through last night..." His voice cracked and it tore at her gut. "I am in *awe* of you."

But she hadn't done anything last night. She'd just

endured. That wasn't brave—that was life.

"And of course there's more for me to learn, so stay…let me get to know all of you."

Eleanor squeezed her eyes shut. *She would not cry.* She couldn't stay. If she did, she wouldn't leave, and this was not the kind of decision they should be making now.

Not twenty-four hours after they'd lost their baby.

She turned to face him. "I need to go home."

"I thought this was your home?"

Eleanor glanced around the cavernous space. It had grown on her, but it didn't feel like her home—not like the farm. *He'd* felt like home. But Bodie was part of the problem at the moment.

"I need my mother right now."

Her voice cracked. She hadn't meant it to. She hadn't even thought about how much she wanted her mother until right now. But *oh,* she did. She yearned for home. It was a different yearning to that which she felt for Bodie, but it was just as strong, just as visceral.

"Christ, Eleanor." He shoved a hand through his hair, defeat in every line of his body. "You're really going to run home to your mother?"

Yeah. She really was. "For now." She nodded. "I need space, Bodie. We *both* do."

The tight line of his shoulders, the erect way he'd been holding himself, suddenly dissolved. "Okay. Fine. I'll…drive you to the airport."

Eleanor supposed she should feel triumphant that he'd seen it her way, but she just felt empty. "I'll get an Uber."

"I can take you to the goddamn airport," he growled, his forehead furrowing.

"I don't want you to."

He stiffened again at her rejection, and Eleanor hated herself for it, but she didn't know if she'd be brave enough to get out of his car once they got there. He'd told her she was brave for enduing the miscarriage, but she hadn't had a choice.

This was a choice. And there was something about an airport that was so final.

"Goodbye, Bodie. I'll ring you in a couple of weeks."

Her heart thundered and her throat burned from holding back the emotion as she brushed past him. But she didn't look back. Just picked up her bags and stepped out of his apartment.

Chapter Fifteen

Bodie stared at the television. He had no idea what was on—some eighties sitcom re-run. It was just background noise to drink to. To try *not* to think to.

It was poker night, but he'd skipped it for the third time in a row. He didn't feel like shooting the shit and smack talking or listening to Linc crap on about women. If anything, since Linc had settled into monogamy, he'd become even more superior about women. Bodie didn't need smug, unsolicited theories on his current poor form with the ball and its correlation to MSP—massive sperm pressure.

Bodie knew exactly why he was playing crap rugby, and while it had everything to do with a woman it had nothing to do with lack of sex. He'd never felt less like doing the wild thing. Not even a little hand relief appealed.

He checked his phone. Again. For the hundred thousandth time since she'd left. In case he'd missed a call or a text. Or she'd posted to Facebook or a blog on her website. *Anything.* Any communication.

But nothing. She'd told him she'd ring, but there'd been

absolute silence.

He was trying not to be a Neanderthal. To give her the time and space she'd asked for. She was grieving, and he'd fucked it all up by blurting out he loved her at probably the worst time possible.

He'd screwed up. He knew that. But as the days passed, the urge to skulk into Bungindally and steal her back was becoming ever more powerful. He missed her and he *loved* her—he *did* love her, despite his crappy timing—and he was tired of doing nothing.

He played rugby. An aggressively take-charge sport. He took the game up to the opposition, he pushed, he *made* things happen.

Sitting around and waiting was not his strong suit.

A sudden thunderous knock on the door dragged him out of the quagmire of self pity. *Ryder.* He didn't need to see his best friend to know it.

Bodie was tempted to tell him to *fuck the fuck off* at the top of his lungs, but he was pathetically needy where Eleanor was concerned. Maybe Ryder had some news of her? *Since he'd asked this morning.*

And every morning for the last three fucking weeks.

He stalked to the front door and yanked it back on its slider. His best friend stood there, cowboy hat pulled low, his big-ass belt buckle shining in the hallway light. He should have looked stupid in the middle of Sydney but somehow he managed to pull it off.

God alone knew what they were going to make of him in Italy, though.

"Shouldn't you be at poker?" Bodie demanded.

"Shouldn't you?"

"I'm busy."

Ryder glanced over at the glass tumbler and the half empty bottle of scotch on the coffee table. "So I see." He held up a plastic shopping bag.

"What's that?"

"It's an intervention. You going to invite me in?"

An inter-*what*? "Hell no." Bodie stood his ground. The last thing he needed was well-intentioned *advice*. He needed a plan to *get her the fuck back*.

Ryder ignored him and pushed inside anyway. He headed straight for the kitchen and helped himself to the cupboard where the tumblers were kept. He crossed to the coffee table, placed the bag down, and poured himself a slug.

Bodie rolled his eyes and headed back to his glass, draining it then pouring himself another before throwing himself down on the couch again.

"So," Ryder said.

Bodie stared at his friend belligerently. "What?"

"You fucked it up."

The fight left his shoulders and he sagged into the couch. "Yeah." He'd fucked it up royally.

"Didn't I tell you not to fuck it up?"

The scotch tasted raw and bitter at the back of Bodie's throat, but he took a decent swallow. "I believe you did."

"And what are you doing about getting her back, because you're a serious fucking downer at the moment, man."

"She wants time. And space. I'm trying to give it to her."

"Did you tell her you love her?"

Bodie thunked his glass down on the table. He wasn't used to a deep and meaningful conversation from Ryder and frankly, it pissed him right off at the moment. "Well fuck man, *that's* what I did wrong."

Ryder grinned. Jesus…he has some stones. "What did she say?"

"She said I didn't know her."

"Exactly." He nodded and picked up the bag. "So I bring you help. You want to know my kooky little sister? It's all in here."

Bodie sat forward, eager but afraid. He'd do anything to get Eleanor back, but it was a very small bag for what seemed a very big problem. "What is it?"

"Books and movies."

"Okay?"

"Chick books. Chick movies. There aren't any explosions. Or car chases or explicit sex."

"No John McClane, I take it?"

Ryder smiled as he shook his head "No Peter Parker, either."

He pulled out a copy of *Pride and Prejudice*. He tossed the book at Bodie, who caught it on reflex.

"I've read Austen."

Ryder laughed. "Of course you have, rich boy. How long ago?"

"In high school." It'd been one of those curriculum books they'd been made to read. But as he flipped through the pages he remembered he may just have looked at the CliffsNotes…

"You want to know who Nell is, what she wants? What she's always wanted? It's in there." Ryder rattled the bag. "In here."

Bodie held out his hand for the nondescript plastic which Ryder handed over. He peered inside. *Emma. Sense and Sensibility. Persuasion. Pride and Prejudice.* A couple of boxed sets of what looked like television dramas. Two more Austen books—*Northanger Abbey* and *Mansfield Park.* Three books by Georgette Heyer.

A fragile flame flickered to life in the darkness of Bodie's soul at the sight of them. Why hadn't he thought of this? She'd told him that first night about her historical romance collection. About her love for Austen and Heyer.

He glanced at Ryder. "Thank you. I know you…I know I'm not what you wanted for your sister."

"Nah, man." Ryder shook his head. "I didn't want my sister to fall in love with some rugby player with a permanent hard-on who only wanted her as a notch on his bedpost. But—" He shrugged. "You love her. Blind fucking Freddy can see that. And you're my best friend. I couldn't think of a better man for her."

Bodie swallowed hard against the block of emotion in his throat. He and Ryder didn't get mushy unless it was after a grand final win. But Ryder's blessing choked him up.

Fuck. He was going to be crying into the copy of *Pride and Prejudice* if he didn't man the fuck up.

"Thanks, dude." Bodie stood and they exchanged an awkward manly shoulder check/hug thing.

Ryder pulled out of it as embarrassed as Bodie. "Just get your shit together. And tell my sister no more scratch marks, okay? That crap makes me want to pluck my eyes out, and I'm not much use to the team blind."

Bodie stayed up till two in the morning reading *Pride and Prejudice*. It took him a week to plough through the rest of the books and all the DVDs. A week to realise what an absolute fucking *idiot* he'd been.

Eleanor was right. He hadn't known her. Not her deepest, truest soul. He'd thought her encyclopaedic interest in the Victorian era was about the frocks and the glamour, a business necessity as well as a barrier for her to hide behind when she was feeling socially awkward.

He hadn't understood that it was more than that.

That Eleanor had marinated in this era of chivalry and romance. Where virginity was prized and people *courted*. Where men formally declared themselves and asked fathers for hands in marriage and fancy wedding feasts followed.

He'd blown all of them.

He'd taken her virginity—although she had been a more-than-willing participant in that. There'd been no courting. No declaration of undying love. No romantic proposal. No asking her father for permission. No fancy ceremony with a stunning dress.

Just an offer of a thirty day wait for a quickie registry office affair.

The pregnancy had taken precedence, and Bodie had favoured expediency over romance. Those things all seemed hopelessly old-fashioned, but he should have known a woman who dressed in corsets and frilly pantaloons and was still a virgin at twenty-six *was* an old-fashioned girl.

That she'd been holding out for *the one*.

Add to that him telling her he loved as if it was some kind of afterthought, some kind of salve for her empty womb. To the woman who'd been holding out for the fairytale?

He really *had* fucked it up.

But he knew how to make it right. Knew he had to make it right. Or at least try. He didn't know if he'd blown it for good. He didn't know if she could forgive his stupid, male, ignorant, clumsy mishandling of it all. Or even if she loved him back. He just knew he had to go and find her and tell her he loved her.

Properly.

It took Bodie another week to put his plans into action. It was the longest week of his life, ending with a rather spectacular black eye from an elbow during the Saturday night game. They won, but Bodie hated that he looked like he'd been in a bar brawl instead of the dapper, contrite *gentleman* he'd been hoping for.

Still, it didn't stop him from getting on the plane to Bungindally on Sunday. Nothing short of a coma could have stopped him. Not even Griff. Thankfully, he'd given Bodie two days off training. Bodie knew he'd pay for them when he got back, but he also knew he would have gone without Griff's permission, so he was happy to have his coach's blessing and take whatever Griff dished out on his return.

Especially if Eleanor said yes.

He wished he could be sure about her feelings. She'd never declared herself as he had. Which could well mean she didn't have feelings for him at all. But she hadn't told him she *didn't* love him that disastrous day he'd blurted out his feelings. And she *had* chosen him to lose her virginity with. *And* left the farm and her life and moved in with him far, far away from her home.

Not to mention how she'd watched all six seasons of *The Walking Dead* with him just because he'd told her how much he loved it. She'd watched through her hands for at least fifty percent of every episode and winced at all the gore and grossness but she'd stuck through all of them. Would she do that for just any guy?

His gut told him no. But it'd been wrong before. And even if she said no, if she *didn't* love him, then he had every intention of *wooing* her. Eleanor deserved what he hadn't thought to give her last time—a good old-fashioned wooing—and unless she told him specifically to take a long run off a short pier, that's exactly what he was going to do.

He didn't know how he'd manage it with his training and game schedule but he'd be out at Bungindally at every opportunity, showing her with his actions and his words that he *did* love her.

That he'd always love her.

It was just after midday when Bodie drove into *Shady Gums*, the Davis property, kicking up clouds of dust with the wheels of his hired car. He'd decided against announcing himself prior. Ryder had assured him that his family should be home as it was the middle of the calving season, so he'd taken a leap of faith that Eleanor and her parents would be in.

As he pulled up at the oasis of green that was the homestead, his confidence wavered. The place seemed quiet. Maybe they were all out tending to newborn calves?

Damn it. He'd psyched himself up and he was ready—he didn't want to hang around for hours waiting for them to return. He wanted to get on with it.

But wait he would. If he had to.

Despite being the middle of winter, the air was warm and dry as he exited the car and he took a second to centre himself and soak in the glorious winter sunshine after a frosty start in Sydney.

The barking of dogs broke the stillness of the air and within seconds he was surrounded by four enthusiastic canines—cattle dogs—all barking happily, licking his hands and wagging their tails. Clearly they were there for their work ethic and not for their guard dog abilities.

"Dogs!" A distant voice called the animals. "C'arn ya all."

Bodie followed the disappearing tails and the voice around the side of the house to find Eleanor's father, John Davis, looking hot and dusty in jeans and long shirt, washing up at a tap. Four wide steps nearby led to the wraparound veranda so typical of Aussie country homesteads.

He straightened when he saw Bodie, a frown crinkling his sweaty forehead, a grimy band of sweat ringing his head where his hat had obviously been sitting. His eyes widened at the long velvet frock coat Bodie was wearing. It had taken him a few days and a not inconsiderate sum of money to buy it from the young designer who'd shown it at the exhibition, but it had been worth every cent.

Even if he did feel like a bloody dill, dressed up like a nineteenth-century earl in the middle of the Australian outback. He'd managed to find some riding breeches and long riding boots, too. He couldn't vouch for the historical accuracy of the accessories but surely she'd give him points for effort?

John quirked an eyebrow. "You're a little too old to be joining the circus."

His drawl was exactly like Ryder's and Bodie laughed. He supposed the clothes were a little like some a ringmaster might wear.

"You should have got a penalty kick for that." He tipped his chin to indicate Bodie's eye.

Bodie shrugged. "Refs. What you going to do?"

There was silence for a beat or two as both men eyed each other warily. "Mr. Davis." He walked closer and extended his hand. "I'm Bodie Webb."

John shook it. "I remember. We met at the party."

"Yes." It had been brief, though, and Bodie wanted to get this right.

"And you got my daughter pregnant then broke her heart."

Bodie's gut dropped at the statement. He hadn't *wanted* to do either. The fact that he'd done the latter, though, was somewhat encouraging.

Would Eleanor be broken-hearted if she didn't care for him?

"Yes." Bodie swallowed, nervousness and anticipation a hard ball in his stomach. "And I have come to apologise. And make things right."

John's gaze drifted to the screen door that opened into the house before returning his attention to Bodie. "Why?"

Bodie shifted. "Because I was an idiot."

The older man folded his arms like he had all the time in the world. "I was thinking more along the lines of dickhead."

"Dickhead definitely fits."

John remained impassive, his inscrutable face lined with years of hard work. He stood there unblinking and patient, rocking back on his heels, *considering.*

A trickle of sweat ran down Bodie's neck. He'd like to blame the warmth of the day but Bodie didn't think his sweating was weather-related.

"I love your daughter, sir, and I know I screwed up, that I did this whole thing back to front, but I've come here today to make that right. To announce my intention to woo, court, and marry Eleanor, sir. I come to seek your permission *and* your blessing to do so."

Long moments passed before the man finally cracked a smile. "You'll do."

Bodie let out a breath through pursed lips, the slick edge of adrenaline dissipating in a flash. He'd thought talking to Eleanor would be the hard part, but this had been nerve-wracking.

"I'm not the one you have to convince, though, am I?"

"No, sir." Bodie's gaze slid to the screen door and back this time. "Is she home?"

John nodded. "In her sewing room. Through the kitchen to the end of the hallway, last door on the left."

Bodie nodded. "Thank you."

"Good luck." John clapped him on the back in a way that led Bodie to believe he was going to need it.

• • •

Eleanor was working on a recent commission, her shoulders hunched over her machine, her tongue caught between her teeth as she concentrated on the tuck that she couldn't get to sit right. The dress had proved to be damn difficult but she relished the challenge.

Anything to occupy her brain at the moment was welcome.

She didn't hear Bodie's footsteps in the hallway. Normally, she'd hear anyone walking her way, as well as cattle calling, cars approaching, dogs barking. But she had earbuds in, listening to an audio version of *Venetia*, one of her favourite Georgette Heyers. The fact that it was read by Richard Armitage was no hardship, either.

He was no Bodie Webb, but…

Gah! Bloody Bodie again.

She'd taken to listening to audiobooks when she worked so she *wouldn't* think about him. Because sewing was so automatic for her, her brain tended to wander. Normally she'd just tune into the sounds of the bush and the farm, but since returning from Sydney it wandered straight to Bodie.

So audiobooks had been a way to distract herself from such thoughts. And from the huge, gaping hole she had in her heart.

Running home to her mother had been restorative in many ways. Her body was back to normal and the unconditional love and support from her family had soothed her aching soul. But it hadn't stopped her wanting Bodie. Hadn't stopped her loving him, either.

Or thinking about him every spare minute of the day.

She didn't know what she was doing, exactly. What she wanted. Or how to go forward with her life. What was she waiting for, for Pete's sake? She loved him. He apparently loved her.

Did it really matter that he told her the way he had?

And yet it did.

God…she was such a cliché… She should be in Sydney,

going after what she wanted. Instead here she was, hiding in the back of beyond, chasing a fairytale in an era that didn't believe in fairytales. Where almost two out of three marriages ended in divorce.

Where happily ever afters were on the endangered list.

Annoyed at the never-ending circular train of her thoughts and her complete inertia, Eleanor forced her attention back to the recalcitrant tuck and the audiobook. But the natural light spilling in from the open wraparound veranda reminded her of Bodie's apartment and her mind drifted to where it shouldn't.

Again.

A short, sharp knock cut through the audio and she lifted her foot off the foot plate. A sudden eerie sensation prickled at her nape and bumped through her heart. She looked over her shoulder.

Bodie.

She blinked. Bodie Webb. *In a frock coat.* In *the* frock coat. And…breeches. And…boots.

And a black eye.

Her pulse fluttered like crazy at her wrists and temples. Had she gone mad? Had she actually conjured him up?

She dragged her gaze back to her Elna before peeking over her shoulder again. He was still there, smiling at her, turning her stomach to jelly.

It *was* him.

If there was any doubt that she loved him, that she'd been swayed by being pregnant and the romanticism of being a family, it completely disintegrated.

"Bodie?"

She stood as if she'd been hit by one of the farm's cattle prods, pulling the ear buds out, blinking at him, trying to assimilate all the clashing thoughts in her head.

God…even with a black eye, he looked amazing. So tall

and broad and sexy in a bloody *frock coat—the* frock coat from the exhibition, she'd know it anywhere—and she was in her faded jeans and a baggy T-shirt, her flyaway hair scraped back in that stupid giant plastic claw that was the ultimate in daggy.

"Hey."

She took a step toward him, frowning at the puffy bruise beneath his eye. "Are you okay?"

He waved a dismissive hand, and she halted. "I'm fine. It's nothing."

"What…" She shook her head, trying to still the pressure of words in her brain all clamouring to get out. "What are you doing here?"

His smile turned lopsided and it was as if a magnetic channel had been opened between the two of them. "You have to ask?"

She nodded.

"I'm here for you."

He strode into the room and walked right up to her, the cut of the coat magnificent on his frame. He reached for her hand and clasped it tight. Eleanor practically swooned at his feet. He'd always been sexy but now he was dashing—the kind of dashing she'd only ever read about.

"You were right. I didn't know you, but I do now. I know that you're a romantic heart, that you want to be wooed and courted. That you want a romantic proposal and a grand wedding with a big dress and a guy who'll ask your father for permission to marry you."

Yes. She did. *Or she had.* All she really wanted now was to climb Bodie like a tree and never let him out of her sight. The rest just *did not* matter. "I don't need it. Not anymore. I just need you."

Bodie shook his head, his indulgent smile cupping her heart in its glow. "Yes you do. And so do I. I've already asked your father for his permission, which just leaves this."

Bodie reached into an inner pocket of the coat and pulled out a small box. He sunk to one knee and Eleanor's heart almost stopped.

"Miss Davis, I love you." He grabbed her left hand and held it in front of him. "They're three pretty simple words and I'm sorry—*so unbelievably sorry*—I screwed them up first time around, but please, *please* believe me, I did mean them when I said them. As I do now. I have loved you since our first night together, and I want to share the rest of my life with you."

He opened the case, and Eleanor gasped at the ring cushioned amidst the rich burgundy velvet. It was a replica of Queen Victoria's engagement ring. She knew that because it was featured in the header of her website, and she had a whole section on her blog devoted to her wedding jewellery.

The gold band was in the shape of a snake, which symbolized eternal love, and the head was set with a deep sparkling emerald, which had been Victoria's birthstone.

"Bodie," she whispered.

"I'm asking you to marry me because it would be my great honour to be your husband, but I need you to know that I'm going to court you first. For as long as you like. And I know that's all ass-backwards, but you deserve it. If you don't want to live together while I do that, hell, if you want to live here during our courtship, then I'll fly back and forth. I'll make it work. If you want to save yourself for our wedding night, I'll make that work, too. And when we finally do get married, I want it to be the biggest and the grandest in the land."

Tears welled in Eleanor's eyes as she stared at the ring. He'd done everything right. Everything her heart had ever desired. The declaration, the getting down on one knee, the perfect ring, asking her father's permission.

He'd even worn a *frock coat.*

"*Bodie*." Her chest was too tight to hold in all the love.

"Will you marry me, Miss Davis?"

"Yes," she whispered, nodding her head, his face blurring before her as tears spilled down her cheeks. "A hundred times yes. I will marry you and court you. I love you."

Bodie let out a long, audible breath and Eleanor laughed. "Thank God," he murmured. "You have no idea how good that is to hear."

Eleanor grinned at him, light as air now the tightness in her chest had evaporated. "Yes. *I do.*"

He took the ring out of its box and slipped it on her finger. It fit perfectly, the emerald in the snake's head glittering in the sunny room. She stared at it. It was hardly desirable as far as modern day engagement rings went, but she was an old-fashioned girl through and through. "You couldn't have picked anything more perfect if you'd tried."

"It might have taken me a while to figure you out, Eleanor Davis, but I'm on your page now."

She pulled her gaze off the ring. He was watching her like…like she was *everything*, and it took her breath away.

"I'm sorry I walked out. I should have stayed. I should have told you I loved you and worked through it. But I didn't trust my feelings. I was so confused and raw and…"

"Shhh." He pressed a finger against her lips. "It's okay. You were right to give us time and space. It wasn't the right time to be making declarations."

He removed his finger then and kissed her. A brief, light brush of his mouth on hers, perfectly chaste in every way. But it jolted like electricity to all her erogenous zones. She mewed when he pulled back. "Is that it?"

He grinned. "Well, a gentleman would never presume in a lady's private chamber."

Eleanor grimaced. "I should have known this was going to come back to bite me."

Bodie laughed and it was such a deep, rich noise, and she'd missed it. "I love your laugh," she said, her finger tracing over his jaw.

"Well, plan on hearing it a lot more, because you make me very, *very* happy, Miss Davis." He bent and kissed her on the mouth, gossamer light, and her eyes fluttered shut. Then his lips brushed the tip of her nose. "Miss Davis." Then they moved to her cheek. "Miss Davis."

Eleanor's eyes opened with a start. "Oh my God, you watched *Pride and Prejudice*?"

"The Keira Knightly one as well as the BBC one." He grinned. "And several other Austen adaptions. As well as three more of her books and quite a few Heyers. She was a bit of saucy minx, wasn't she?"

Eleanor smiled, sliding her arms around his neck and raising herself on her tippy toes. "Speaking of saucy minxes."

"Why, Miss Davis, this isn't appropriate behav—"

Eleanor yanked on his neck to cut him off. "Shut up and kiss me."

And he did. A *very* twenty-first century kiss. But there were advantages to living in modern times, and Eleanor planned to exploit them thoroughly.

Their happily ever after started today.

Glossary

I've probably used some words in here that some readers may not know—both rugby ones and strange Aussie-isms alike. So I thought a handy dandy glossary might help. It is, of course, written entirely from my perspective so is heavily biased, female-centric, and quite possibly dodgy. It probably wouldn't stand up to any kind of official scrutiny…

Footy—We love this term in Australia. The confusing thing for most non-Aussies is they never know which game it refers to because we have three separate but distinct codes of football in Australia:

1. Rugby League (Jarryd Hayne played this code before he went and played Gridiron).

2. Rugby union—The code the Sydney Smoke play and the one this series is based upon (Jarryd Hayne tried his hand at this code for a bit after the whole Gridiron thing didn't work out but is now back playing League).

3. Aussie rules football—Different altogether. Tall, fit guys in *really* tight shorts.

There is also soccer but we don't really think of that as football in the traditional sense here in Australia.

The confusing thing is we refer to all of them as *the footy*, e.g. "Wanna go to the footy, Davo?" And somehow we all seem to know which code is being referred to at any given time. Even more confusing, the ball that is used in each code is often also called *the footy*, e.g. "Chuck me the footy, Gazza."

Pitch—Apparently the rugby field is called a pitch but colloquially here we just call it the footy (see, I told you we liked that term) field. A pitch is more a cricket term. No, don't worry, I won't ever try to explain a game that lasts five days to you...

Ruck—No, not a typo. That's ruck with an *R*, ladies! Happens after a tackle as each team tries to gain possession of the ball.

Line-out—That weird thing they use to restart play where each team lines up side by side, vertical to the sideline, and one of the guys throws the ball to his team and a few of the guys from that team bodily lift one dude up to snatch the ball out of the air. It's like rugby ballet. Minus the tutus. And usually with more blood.

Scrum—Another way to gain possession of the ball. I'm going to paraphrase several definitions I've read: A scrum is when two groups of opposing players pack loosely together, arms interlocked, heads down, jockeying for the ball that is fed into the scrum along the ground. It's like a tug of war with no rope and more body contact or, as I like to call it, a great big man hug with a lot of dudes lying on top of each other at the end of it all. Very homoerotic. Win/win.

Maul—The good kind. It's when at least three rugby players from either side—one with the ball—are in contact together to challenge possession. Yes, another man hug! Sounds positively delicious, doesn't it?

Try—A goal. Except in rugby union we don't say someone scored a goal, we say someone scored a try after they've dived for the line and a bunch of other guys have jumped on top to try and stop it from happening. Very homoerotic. Win/win. A try is worth five points.

WAGs—Wives and girlfriends. These are partners of the dudes that play rugby. Although we also use the term here in Oz to refer to partners of our cricket players. I think in the UK WAGs is also a term used for football (soccer) partners.

Akubra—An iconic Australian brand of hat worn by country guys and gals. Vaguely similar to the Stetson but I'll probably have my nationality revoked for saying so! It has a distinctive shape that's about as Aussie as vegemite.

Arvo—In that long tradition of shortening everything and sticking an *O* on the end, this is Aussie for afternoon, eg. "Hey Robbo, whatcha doin' this arvo?"

Wank—To wank is to masturbate. Pretty much always referring to a guy. Although we embrace all terms for this biological process. Jerking/jacking/tossing off are well known, as are spanking the monkey and choking the chicken (or chook as we say here). There's also the term wanker which is actually rarely used to describe one who wanks. We much prefer to use this as an insult for someone who is a bit of a jerk, eg. "That Johnno is a wanker."

Boardies—Shortened (of course) from board shorts, the knee-length shorts worn to the beach by blokes, although women wear them as well.

Togs—Some Aussies call swimming suits togs. No one knows why.

Starkers—Completely, utterly, 100 percent naked.

Bum bag—Known as fanny packs in the USA. But a fanny here in Australia is a "front bottom" on a woman and none of us can keep a straight face calling them that…

Hard yakka—Yakka is work. So, any job that's heavy or difficult or requires muscle is hard yakka. Also a rugged brand of clothing designed to survive said yakka.

Cattle station/property—A farm or a ranch where cattle (and sheep) are raised. Usually has to be a big-ass property to be considered a station. When someone's taking a betting game too serious here, we'll often say, "Come on, Richo, we're not playing for sheep stations."

Woop woop—Out in the middle of bloody nowhere. Usually where you can find most cattle stations!

Out past the black stump—another way of saying woop woop. No, nobody knows where the black stump is exactly…

Jackaroo—a station hand on farm/station/property. In other words, an Aussie cowboy. Yeehaw!

Softdrink—this is what we call a soda. Soft refers to it being non-alcoholic/wussy.

Ute—Short (just for something different) for utility vehicle. Similar to the pickup.

Fair dinkum—Slang for something that is true or genuine. "Fair dinkum, mate, that bloody cattle station out woop woop got six inches of rain last night."

Cooee—An Aussie bush call used to attract attention. Or a way of describing how near or far something is. "I was within bloody cooee of Bazza." Or "I wasn't in bloody cooee of Bazza."

Yobbo—An uncouth individual. Or Aussie for dickhead.

Dill—an affectionate term for a fool/idiot. "Don't mind Robbo, he's a bit of a dill."

Trackie daks—trackie refers to a tracksuit and daks refers to trousers. So these are tracksuit bottoms. Generally not the most sophisticated choice of clothing, usually just something to slop around the house in.

Dag/daggy—a dag actually refers to the matted wool around a sheep's ass but we also apply it to people, usually affectionately. A person can be "a dag" which means someone who's funny but not very hip or fashionable. And you can "look daggy" by wearing your oldest/ill fitting/ill-kept/out-of-fashion clothes (trackie daks is a classic example) and generally just not really care about how you look.

Acknowledgments

My thanks, as always, go to the team at Brazen. A hell of a lot of work goes on behind the scenes to get these fabulous books into your hands and it's much appreciated. Special thanks to Riki Cleveland and Shayla Fereshetian and everyone in publicity and marketing and to Curtis Svehlak for being my go-to guy.

As always, to Liz Pelletier for her collaboration, her cheerleading, her faith and her editing insights. She knows when to give me free reign and when to reel me in. She "gets" me and that's a true gift in an author/editor relationship. Extra thanks to Hannah Lindsay for her copy editing and coping with my eye wincing penis references.

Thanks to my Austen fan club women—Rachael Bailey, Jodi McAlister, and Clare Connelly—your insights were valuable. And to David Grice and Jon O'Brien, who continue to promptly answer my crazy rugby questions with head-spinning thoroughness. It's nice to have a couple of gurus on speed dial.

About the Author

Multi-award-winning and *USA Today* bestselling author Amy Andrews is an Aussie who has written fifty romances, from novellas to category to single title in both the traditional and digital markets for a variety of publishers. Her first love is steamy contemporary romance that makes her readers tingle, laugh, and sigh. At the age of sixteen, she met a guy she instantly knew she was going to marry, so she just smiles when people tell her insta-love books are unrealistic because she did marry that man and, twenty-odd years later, they're still living out their happily ever after.

She loves good books, fab food, great wine, and frequent travel—preferably all four together. She lives on acreage on the outskirts of Brisbane with a gorgeous mountain view but secretly wishes it were the hillsides of Tuscany.

Discover the* Sydney Smoke Rugby *series…

PLAYING BY HER RULES

PLAYING IT COOL

PLAYING THE PLAYER

PLAYING WITH FOREVER

Also by Amy Andrews

NO MORE MR. NICE GUY

ASK ME NICELY

TAMING THE TYCOON

THE COLONEL'S DAUGHTER

'TIS THE SEASON TO BE KISSED

HANKY-SPANKY CHRISTMAS

If you love sexy romance, one-click these steamy Brazen releases…

Scoring with the Wrong Twin

a *WAGS* novel by Naima Simone

Shy Sophia Cruz has a hard time telling her vivacious identical twin "no." But when her sister begs her to swap places for a modeling shoot, she caves. She's determined to keep things professional with gorgeous Zephirin Black of the Washington Warriors. But when one day turns into one night…and then another, she finds it harder and harder to keep her secret. But coming clean to once-burned-twice-shy Zeph will mean losing him for good.

Sweet Attraction

a *Slow Seductions* novel by Melanie Munton

When Jade Hollingsworth's first ever—and toe-curlingly awesome—one-night stand turns out to be the elusive contractor she hired to remodel the beachwear shop she bought sight-unseen, her plans for a brand new life in a brand new town threaten to go up in flames…the ones ignited by their affair. Hunter Sparks is one bad boy she needs to steer clear of…but it would be much easier if he'd keep his hands to himself.

29457744R00134

Printed in Great Britain
by Amazon